Love, Lies & Consequences Trilogy

Book Three : Consequences

By

Susan Elle

For

Ursula Publishing UK

Love, Lies & Consequences
Book Three : Consequences
Text Copyright © 2013
By Susan Elle
Ursula Publishing UK
All Rights Reserved.

Cover Photograph
© Yuri Arcurs/Dreamstime.com

ISBN 978-1-910753-07-1

Other Books by Susan Elle

The Sara Colson Trilogy includes

Sara's Child

Sara's Loss

Sara's Shame

All the above also available as audio books.

Catherine Colson-Sayers Investigations

CCS Investigations : Bk 1 : Missing

CCS Investigations : Bk 2 : The Chosen

CCS Investigations : Bk 3 : Travis

CCS Investigations : Bk 4 : Deleted

CCS Investigations : Bk 5 : Mind Games, due out end
Aug 2015, twice the length of previous books.

Tempest

Broken

Love, Lies & Consequences Trilogy

Love : Bk1

Lies : Bk2

Consequences : Bk3

Langdon Trilogy

Heart & Home : Bk1

Heart of a Lion : Bk2

Heart of Stone : Bk3

www.susan-elle.com

Table of Contents

PROLOGUE

Stretching lazily, Palmer's lean muscled body feels languid and sated after a night of passion in the arms of the woman he loves.

Turning on to his back, he opens his eyes and immediately senses that something is wrong.

Leaning up on his elbows, Palmer looks over to the spot near the windows where Zoe loves to look out over the city, but she isn't there.

Turning his head to the bed where she had lain next to him, Palmer spots the note that Zoe has left for him.

Dropping on to his back, he reads the note then balls it up and throws it across the empty room.

Damn it, Zoe! Couldn't you have given me some time to put things right, to prove I'm not the man those letters made me out to be!

But she's gone, and Palmer has to get his act together if he's going to find out who is behind his run of bad luck.

CHAPTER ONE

"Are you sure you want to be here?" Tara asks Zoe on her first morning back working in the florist shop.

"Thanks for the concern, but this is exactly where I want to be," Zoe assures her boss, who has become somewhat of a friend.

"Well, I can't say I'm not glad to have you back," Tara grins happily. "You know what the workload is like around here. I just wish things could have worked out better for you."

Nodding, and continuing to wrap individual flowers to make buttonholes for a wedding, Zoe considers before answering.

"I think things turned out as well as could be expected in the circumstances," she sighs. "And at least I got to see my mum again – it was wonderful to see her, though she nagged me, of course."

"About coming back here?" Tara asks.

Zoe nods and frowns, "She wants me close by because of the baby – and she misses me too. But I told her, I can manage. And I have a good life here, now."

Tara sits nearby and looks at Zoe with concern in her eyes. "I know you're not a stupid woman, but I'm going to say this anyway," she smiles tentatively. "Babies are hard work. The more support you can muster to ease the load, the better your life will be."

"I'll manage. I have to," Zoe purses her lips in a determined smile. "It was my choice to continue with this pregnancy and I don't regret it one bit."

"In my own clumsy way, I'm just telling you that I'm here if you need me," Tara reaches across the workbench to take one of Zoe's busy hands. "You have a friend as well as an employer – I just want you to know that."

Giving Tara's fingers a friendly squeeze, Zoe nods and smiles. "I appreciate that more than I can tell you. The people here have been friendly to me, but getting to know people and making real friends is bound to take time."

"Hmm, you're going to antenatal classes I take it?" Tara asks.

"Yes, they're really helpful. I know nothing about having a baby or looking after one," Zoe chuckles uncertainly.

"Don't you chat with the other mums?" Tara asks with a frown.

A tint of pink stains her cheeks as Zoe concentrates on the carnation she is working on. "They seem to know each other already."

"Hmm, when's your next class?"

"6:30 tomorrow night. I'm not really looking forward to it, but I'll go because they're so full of helpful information."

"Fine! Do you want to pick me up or should I pick you up?" Tara asks firmly.

"You...you'd come with me? But what about your children – evenings must be busy for you what with getting their tea and putting them to bed?" Zoe asks Tara, but is already looking forward to her company.

"Nothing my hubby can't handle," Tara insists. "He's great, and the kid's like him reading their bedtime story. Apparently he makes them scarier than I do," she rolls her eyes and laughs.

Zoe drives as little as possible these days. Her pregnancy is progressing well and she doesn't want to take unnecessary risks. And besides, it's becoming too uncomfortable trying to fit behind the wheel.

Waiting for Tara to pick her up for the antenatal class, Zoe fusses around the cottage too nervous to sit still.

I don't know why I'm so nervous – I'm usually good at making new friends. It's just...somehow this is different. I'm an outsider. A foreigner, as they call us interlopers. But I'm doing my best to fit in.

When the doorbell rings it makes Zoe jump and she puts a hand to her racing heart.

"Hey, you ok?" Tara asks when Zoe opens the door to her.

Chuckling, Zoe nods and locks the front door before following Tara to her car.

"I was in a world of my own and the doorbell made me jump, that's all."

"Worrying about tonight, I'll bet," Tara guesses correctly, and smiles when she sees Zoe blush. "Well stop it! We might not greet newcomers with open arms but we draw the line at eating them for supper. Ok?"

Smiling at her own silliness, Zoe nods and climbs into the passenger side of Tara's car.

Walking into the antenatal class 10 minutes later, Zoe and Tara cross the room and take a seat next to 3 mums sat chatting together.

"Hi...," Tara smiles broadly, "...you look like you're almost there."

The proud woman sat next to Zoe puts a hand to her very prominent abdomen and returns Tara's smile.

"Just two weeks left, then I'll be putting all this stuff into practice," she tells them. Then she turns more towards Zoe, "I've noticed you before, you're not from round here are you?"

Grimacing, Zoe shakes her head. "No, but I am permanent," she adds hopefully, and gets a chuckle by way of reply.

"Well that makes all the difference," the woman tells Zoe. "I'm Carole, this is Emma and that's Pat; they're not as far along as me so you'll see them for a while yet."

The other two women lean forward and offer Zoe a smile. "Hi, I'm Zoe, and I'll be here for a while yet too. I'm only 23 weeks along," she tells them.

"Same as me, then," Pat holds out a hand to Zoe. "We'll be able to compare notes on how things are going."

"That would be great! I know nothing about all of this, so the classes are a necessity for me. Do you have any other children," Zoe asks her new friend.

Shaking her head, Pat grimaces," No, it's my first too. I don't like the look of the birthing, but I suppose the outcome is worth the pain."

Returning her grimace, Zoe agrees, "I'll be glad when that part is over. Still, we have a while before we need to worry about it."

Laughing, the women all chatter for another few minutes until the Midwife calls the class to order and begins the session.

"That wasn't so bad, was it," Tara states with a smile when they both climb back into her car.

Returning the smile, Zoe shakes her head, "Thanks to you I now have 3 new friends and won't be worried about going to the next class. You are such a good friend, I'm so lucky to have found you."

Shifting uncomfortably in her seat, Tara starts the car and begins the drive home.

"Don't talk wet, I just broke the ice," Tara dismisses with a sigh. "You would have made friends soon enough – I just smoothed the way so you wouldn't give up on the classes."

"Well, I appreciate it," Zoe says sincerely. "I'm not usually backwards at coming forwards, but this is different. I'm a stranger in a strange place and people are bound to regard me as such."

"You're strange alright," Tara laughs.

Zoe joins in the laughter and says, "Hey! You're supposed to be my friend – if you think I'm strange what does everyone else think!"

"Honestly...," Tara turns briefly to look at Zoe, "...the people who mention anything at all have been extremely sympathetic. They know you haven't got an easy future ahead of you."

"Oh!"

"Cornish folk are family oriented. The idea of you coping alone is frankly puzzling to them," Tara explains.

"Hmm, my mum couldn't understand my choice either," Zoe admits. "But I didn't feel that I had a choice. Of course I would love to have my mum's support through all of this – but it was breaking my heart to be around Palmer. I love him just as much as ever, even now."

It takes Palmer a long time to pull himself together and get on with his day. But he knows, if he is to stand any chance of winning Zoe back for good, he needs to clear his name.

He decides to take a further look at Snelson, the building contractor who had won most of the tenders where his had inexplicably failed.

It's not that he believed he should have won all of those contracts, but with his previous track record he had expected to win at least half.

By deciding to give the Hambling PI Agency a try, Palmer was killing two birds with one stone. He could find out more about the agency where Thomas Grady had worked and maybe some more about what his duties were.

An hour later he walked into their reception and caused a stir. Tall and lean, his firm body was shown off to perfection in the fitted white shirt and black trousers he wore.

The two girls talking at the reception desk fell silent and one had her mouth open. Receiving a dig in the ribs from the other woman the younger woman closed her mouth then opened it to welcome Palmer and ask if she could help him.

"As a matter of fact..."

"Bye girls...," a man calls as he crosses the reception to the main door, "...I'll be back before closing to pick up my messages." And then he was gone.

With pursed lips the receptionist shakes her head and makes a note on the pad in front of her. She wrote the time and a man's name then the fact that he wouldn't be in till later.

"So that's Tom Grady?" Palmer asks, causing both girls to blink in surprise. When they eventually nod he tells them, "That's a shame, I was hoping to hire him. He came highly recommended."

Breaking into a relieved smile the younger woman tells Palmer not to worry. "We have a lot of very experienced investigators on our staff. Would you like me to make an appointment for you to meet one of them?"

"Hmm, I was hoping to get something sorted right now." Then looking directly into her wide brown eyes, he tells her, "My brother just died – he was the one who hired Mr Grady, and I want to find out as much as I can about the time before his death."

Then, to clear the way for his next request, Palmer states, "I have the unpleasant duty of being my brother's executor, so legally I have to clear up his bank and business dealings. To do that properly I need to know what Connor was doing prior to his death." And with a look of deep concern and sorrow he adds, "He was only 24, they beat him almost to death and left him in the street to die alone."

He hadn't said anything that wasn't true, but he watches the appalled look on their young faces turn to concern.

"Oh, you poor man," the young receptionist says with a tear in her voice, then looks up to the slightly older woman at her side. "We need to help, Stacy. It's our legal and moral duty," she states, turning back to Palmer for confirmation.

And with his nod, Stacy agrees, "Ok. But if I show you the file you can never tell anyone I did so."

Palmer immediately agrees, hardly daring to believe his luck.

But when Stacy comes back a full five minutes later she actually hands him the file.

Looking left and right before handing it to him, Stacy says, "I made you a copy of everything, but if anyone ever finds out I would lose my job."

"You girls are the best," Palmer states, and gives them a killer-watt smile that almost has them swooning. Then, leaning over the desk, he kisses first the girl who is sitting and then Stacy, who remains standing, but not for long after she receives her kiss on the lips.

For the rest of that day the two girls giggle and talk about the handsome stranger that they had helped and the kiss he'd given them as a reward.

But Palmer has moved on to more serious matters and is soon reading the reports that Grady had copied for his file.

Before he can finish the one about Grady finding Zoe, Palmer's mobile starts to ring.

"Craig, what's up..." he asks, not really thinking anything was wrong, but his face pales when he hears the big man's reply. "Jesus! I'll be right there. Was anyone injured?"

Listening to Craig, Palmer pushes an agitated hand back through his hair and groans.

"Thank God for that! I'll be on-site in half an hour —

I'm leaving right now!" With that, Palmer shoves his mobile into his trouser pocket then snatches up his car keys and bolts out of his loft door.

The architect, Terry Fielding, greets Palmer as soon as he arrives on site.

"There's considerable damage to the building but nothing that can't be repaired. And, thank the Lord, Sean wasn't badly hurt – more shaken up than anything."

Both men stride across the building site and over to where Sean is being treated by paramedics.

"Sean, are you alright," Palmer demands.

"Sorry boss, I don't know what happened," Sean tells him while nodding his answer. "I was using the forklift to move some of the bricks and it wouldn't stop. I kept pumping the brake but it wouldn't stop," he repeats desperately.

Turning to the paramedics, Palmer asks, "Does he need the hospital?"

"No. Thankfully he was wearing a hard hat and his injuries are superficial, though no doubt painful," the younger man tells Palmer. "However, I wouldn't recommend that he continue to work after such a shock – when it sinks in what could have happened he won't be thinking straight and that's never good on a building site."

When Sean makes to protest, Palmer holds up a

staying hand. "You'll go home and take the rest of the week off with pay. And if you still don't feel right by Monday you call in and we'll sort it from there. No heroics, you got me!"

"Yes boss," Sean grimaces as one of the lacerations to his arm is cleaned and dressed.

"Now stay here and wait for me to arrange transport – I don't want you driving yourself!"

One look at his boss's face tells Sean not to bother arguing and he nods instead.

"Good man!"

Together, Palmer and Terry move to the damaged wall and inspect the damage.

"This will need to come down completely, but there's no other damage so the financial cost should be minimal," Terry tells him.

"At this minute, I'm more interested in the human cost," Palmer sighs heavily, pushing a hand back through his blond hair as he surveys the damage.

The forklift was carrying a full palette of bricks so had acted as a battering ram when it wouldn't stop. Stepping up to the cab, Palmer notes that the keys have been removed.

"I'm going to contact the plant hire company and demand this vehicle be thoroughly inspected," Palmer says as he jumps down. "I want to know why a forklift that has been working perfectly suddenly fails."

Terry frowns, his eyes full of concern. "Are you thinking this could have been deliberate?"

Before Palmer can answer, Craig comes striding across from the port-a-cabin that acts as the site office.

"I think we should take this inside," Craig suggests, glancing his eyes round at the men standing nearby.

"You're right, let's go," Palmer agrees and Terry accompanies the two men into the office.

Closing the door, Palmer naturally moves behind the main desk and takes a seat, waiting for the other two to seat themselves.

"What's going on, Craig? You obviously have some ideas..." Palmer observes while eyeing his friend curiously.

Craig's deep, gravelly voice rolls out on a sigh. "Hmm...you could say that." Then the big man gets to his feet, needing something to do, and makes the three of them some coffee. "I don't believe this is the first incident..."

"What!?"

"Just hear me out," Craig demands as he retakes his seat. "I didn't realise it at the time, but there have been a few smaller incidents that could have been put down to carelessness or sheer stupidity – and I already balled the men concerned out so you don't need to do it again," he warns when Palmer looks angrily out the window to where his men have taken up their tools again.

"The incident before this was a cross-wired drill that Scott Freeman was about to use," Craig shakes his large head and gives another deep sigh. "Scott, as you know, is an experienced man who checks his tools before he uses them. When he noticed that the plug had been tampered with he undid it and found the crossed wires."

"And you didn't think to tell me about this?" Palmer asks, incredulous at the thought of what might have happened.

"I took care of it," Craig states firmly. "You had a lot of other stuff on your plate – Connor being just one of them." He watches Palmer nod in acknowledgement then continues.

"I had all the electrical equipment brought in here and Scott and I checked them out before anyone used them – we found two more cross-wired," he states, looking from Palmer to Terry and back again.

"Jesus!" Getting to his feet, Palmer begins to pace the office. "This has got to be Jennings! There's no one else who would put the men's lives at risk that way!"

"Jennings...who's Jennings...?" Terry asks, concerned to hear that the 'accident' was almost certainly a deliberate act.

Craig looks to Palmer and waits for him to explain.

"My brother, Connor, got into debt to a hood named Jennings," Palmer tells Terry. "I paid it off but something must have happened because we believe it was one of his men that beat Connor so badly that it cost him his life."

"You...he..." Putting his coffee down before he spills it, Terry Fielding has to pull himself together. "You think this gangster had Connor killed and is targeting you and your men?!"

Nodding, Palmer looks back to Craig, "I think that's a good bet, yes. But why now?"

Looking up at his boss and friend, Craig is loath to add to his troubles. "I hear the police paid Jennings a call...actually took him into the station and grilled him for a time."

Turning his face up to the ceiling, Palmer closes his eyes with a groan. "So this is my fault. If I hadn't given them Jennings' name none of this would have happened!"

"You had no other choice...," Craig tells him angrily, "...so stop blaming yourself for something you couldn't have stopped!"

"I'm getting night security in place before end of day! And I want to hear about any other incidents, no matter how small, is that clear?!"

Glaring as only Craig can, he nods his large head and bites his tongue on an angry retort.

<u>CHAPTER TWO</u>

By the time Friday comes, Palmer has the security in place on all three of his construction sites.

Craig had thought he was going overboard to install security at the two smaller, almost finished sites, but Palmer had been adamant.

Now he's ready for a break.

Craig is in charge and will tell him of any problems; time to spend some time trying to sort out his personal life.

If Zoe thinks that going back to Looe is going to keep me away she can think again! I'm not letting go of the only woman I've ever loved, or ever want to love!

The drive down to Looe is long and hard after a full day of trying to solve the mystery of Connor's death and his dealings with the private eye, Grady. But it gives him time to mull over a few things, though he doesn't like where his thoughts are taking him.

Thanks to Grady's obsessional record keeping, I have a copy of all the reports he did while working for Connor.

Christ, Connor, you were following her right from the off – did you have to have everything that was mine, even Zoe?

Bashing his hand against the steering wheel, Palmer tries to calm his anger.

If you'd just told me how unhappy you were we could have worked something out. Why the hell didn't you trust me – it didn't have to be this way!

Hitting a bottleneck at Boston, Palmer is sat in traffic for over an hour, just barely moving.

Thank god for air-con, this is crazy!

When the traffic jam suddenly dissipates, Palmer finds himself wondering what the holdup had been. But he's just glad to be back underway.

Even though it's now 7pm he seems to have come through some rush-hour traffic.

Commuters, probably. Though hell knows where they work to be still on their way home at this time of day.

By the time he reaches the toll bridge across the River Tamar and into Saltash, Palmer is glad to be almost there.

Zoe...it's good to feel that you're somewhere nearby. I can't wait to see you!

Going straight to Tara's house, he gently knocks on the front door and waits.

It's Tara's husband, Brian, who opens the door to him, someone Palmer has never met.

"Sorry, I know it's late, and I know I'm a stranger to you, but it's really important that I speak with Tara, Zoe's boss," he clarifies when the man holding the front door open looks ready to slam it in his face.

"Yew soas o' Zoe's, a' ee?" he asks instead, confusing Palmer for a moment with his broad Cornish accent.

"Soas...?" Palmer gapes nonplussed.

"It means friend," Tara says, coming up behind her husband. "I'll deel wi' thus," she tells Brian as she moves past him, then turns to invite Palmer in with a wave of her hand.

"I'll av a leak ov tay ef es gwain," Brian tells Tara as she shows Palmer into the back room.

Once Palmer is seated at the breakfast table, Tara puts the kettle on to make them all a cup of tea.

"Does Zoe know you're here," she asks Palmer with a concerned frown.

"No, not yet," he tells her, glad that Tara's accent is so much easier to understand. "That's sort of why I'm here — I don't have her actual address. The last time I saw Zoe in Looe was in this very house and we just didn't get around to talking about it back in Birmingham."

Turning back to making the tea, Tara pours a little of the boiled water into the empty teapot to warm it, then tips it down the sink. Putting a couple of scoops of loose leaf tea into the pot, she pours on the boiling water and leaves it to steep.

"I haven't seen tea made that way ever," Palmer smiles, delighted by the old tradition.

"I suppose you use teabags in cups," Tara tuts reproachfully. "You'll soon taste the difference," she tells him, taking a tea-strainer out of a drawer and pouring him a cup through it.

"There you go," she says, putting a lovely cup and saucer in front of Palmer then taking another through to Brian.

"That's amazing," Palmer's brows lift as he tastes the steaming brew.

"Uhuh, it's never the same when you use those teabags that so many people buy these days," she grimaces as she takes her tea and sits opposite him at the table. "There's sugar if you take it?"

"No...," Palmer shakes his head, "...this is fine. Thank you."

Watching him over her teacup, Tara's frown of concern returns.

"What is it you want from me, Palmer? You could have waited till the morning outside the florist shop and found Zoe that way," she states bluntly. "And you can't seriously expect me to believe that you would call on Zoe at this time of night – it would frighten the poor girl to death!"

With pursed lips, Palmer nods in agreement. "Yes, it would, I realise that. And you're right when you say I could have found her myself in the morning," he admits hesitantly.

"So why are you really here?" Tara watches Palmer closely, her eyes boring into his soul as if to see the truth for herself.

Dragging in a huge breath, Palmer lets it go in a long sigh. "I don't know how to get through to Zoe, how to prove that I'm innocent of whatever the photos show me doing," he tells her with his palms held upwards in a helpless gesture.

"Apparently they show me kissing some woman that I know nothing about," he expands when Tara remains silent. "But I didn't, I haven't kissed anyone but Zoe since the day we met, and probably a couple of months or so before that!"

Not taking her eyes away from his, Tara asks, "Then how do you explain the existence of such photos."

Sighing again, Palmer pushes both hands back through his hair but doesn't break the important eye contact with Tara.

"I have no idea where they came from, or how they come to have a date stamp on them that puts me squarely in the wrong," he tells her, his frustration hard to control. "That's why I need to see Zoe. I need to see those photos to know what I'm up against."

Then he does something purely instinctual, Palmer reaches across the table to take Tara's hand and feels an unexpected tingle go up his arm.

"Please, help me. I love Zoe more than life. I can't lose her over something I never did!"

Still Tara doesn't speak, but places the hand Palmer had reached across the table between both of her palms.

The tingle up his arm becomes a warm sensation that has his eyes opening wide. Then he sees her nod and smile as she releases his hand.

"I will help you – you have a very pure heart," she tells him mystically.

"I don't know what you just did, but if it convinced you to help me I'm all for it," Palmer grins appreciatively.

"The Celtic Cornish folk have many gifts and traditions," Tara tells him, while explaining nothing at all.

"Then I can only be thankful that Zoe found her way to you," his smile hopeful.

"Yes, I've often wondered about that," Tara muses while sipping her tea. "She has a natural talent for creating beautiful things – she too has a very pure heart." Then she frowns and looks away.

"What? What's wrong?"

"Nothing is wrong," Tara tells him while clearing away their cups. "But... It's nothing. Just a feeling I got, that's all."

But Palmer won't let it go. "A feeling – as in when you were holding my hand?"

Chuckling softly, Tara places the cups into the sink then comes back to sit opposite Palmer.

"You probably think it's all hocus pocus," she grins.

"No..." Palmer shakes his head, his eyes intent upon hers, "...before just now, maybe. But I felt the tingle and warmth flow up my arm and into my heart, whatever it is you do it's real," he declares sincerely.

Nodding, Tara holds out her hand palm up across the table and waits for Palmer to lay his over it. Then she covers his with her other hand and looks deep into his eyes and in to his soul.

"Sometimes, souls are so perfectly matched that they find each other lifetime after lifetime, forever and always," she tells him quietly. "I've only ever felt one soul as pure as yours and it belongs to Zoe, your eternal wife, for want of a better word."

Leaving his hand between hers he asks, "So you'll help me? You'll help us to resolve this barrier between us?"

Nodding, Tara simply says, "I will."

When Zoe gets to work the next morning, she finds Tara working at the counter and singing a lilting tune to herself.

"That's beautiful," she declares with a wide, happy smile.

"It's a tune my grandmother used to sing to me when I was a babe," Tara tells her.

"That was a strange language you were using, where does it come from?"

"It's Kernewek," Tara smiles, happy to share something of her heritage. "My grandmother taught me the words and some of the old language."

"You speak Kernewek...?" Zoe gapes her eyes going wide.

"Not really. I just know the basics, and of course Brian is fairly fluent having been brought up by his Kernewek speaking grandparents," Tara informs her.

"Wow. Does he do anything to keep the language alive," Zoe asks with genuine interest.

"As a matter of fact he does," Tara states proudly. "He teaches a class at the local community centre, and it's grown over the years."

When the shop doorbell chimes to notify them of a customer, Zoe turns to greet them and comes face to face with Palmer.

"You!" she shouts in a shocked and accusatory manner.

"Well hi to you too," he grins sheepishly.

Looking from Palmer to Tara, Zoe detects a conspiracy. "You knew," she accuses Tara directly. "I can tell. You knew he was here and you didn't even warn me!"

Smiling, Tara isn't concerned by her vexed attitude at all. "I did, I admit it. But I wanted to give Palmer the chance to tell you himself."

Frowning and shaking her head in disbelief, Zoe turns back to Palmer. "You cannot be here! You need to get back in your fancy car and go back to Birmingham where you belong!"

But Palmer is already shaking his head. "No can do," he tells her with a smile. "I'm not here to bother you; I'm staying in a local hotel, so there's no pressure. I just want the chance to spend some time with the woman I love. The woman I believe still loves me," he tells her, tilting his head to one side and giving her his best killer smile.

"That's not fair!" she exclaims petulantly. "You know I still have feelings for you – do you think I would have jumped into bed with you otherwise." Then realising that they are not alone, Zoe blushes and turns to apologise to Tara.

"Sorry about that, I just meant..." *Damn it! What exactly do I mean?! I can't get this man out of my head or my heart, that's why I needed to come back here. Now here he is forcing himself back into my life – what the heck am I supposed to do now?!*

Lifting her hands and letting them fall in a helpless gesture, Zoe finally turns back to Palmer and says, "Well you can't stay here, I'm working," and lifts her chin in triumph.

But Tara has other ideas. "Actually, I don't really need you today. We're all caught up on the back orders – what we've got on the books now I can manage with Donna."

Floundering, Zoe looks at Tara with her jaw hanging open in shock. "I thought you told me Donna left just before I started? Does this mean I no longer have a job," she asks, her eyes pleading for it not to be true.

But Tara shakes her head, "Not at all; Donna just let me know that she's available to do a few hours if I get stuck. Between you and me, I think they're struggling for money with the new baby coming along. And she was always reliable and quite good at making up the arrangements."

Somehow that doesn't make Zoe feel any better.

Perhaps with Donna back on the scene, Tara will gradually give her more and more hours making Zoe's contribution unnecessary.

"Is it because I'm pregnant," she asks forlornly.

Coming from behind the counter, Tara gives Zoe a warm hug. "You still have a job here if you want it. I'm just trying to help a friend out too." Looking over Zoe's shoulder, Tara winks at Palmer.

"Maybe it will give you time to take some rest now that you're getting heavier," Palmer suggests, and earns a scowl from Zoe as she spins to face him.

"What exactly are you trying to say," she demands heatedly.

Holding his hands up with palms out, Palmer pleads innocence. "Nothing. Not a thing." But when she continues to scowl at him, he adds, "I just want to spend some time with you, Zoe. Is that such a crime?"

Her scowl gradually fades and a reluctant smile tugs at the corners of her lips. "I don't suppose so being as you're already here," she capitulates, then turns back to her boss. "Are you really sure about this? I can stay until lunch time then spend some time with Palmer," she offers, but Tara won't hear of it.

"Get off with you both, before I really do change my mind," Tara grins, holding the shop door open and shooing them out of it.

CHAPTER THREE

Only when she was walking towards the beach with Palmer did Zoe allow herself to acknowledge that she had missed him terribly.

They weren't exactly holding hands, but they were walking too close together to be just friends.

"So, how's everything going," Palmer asks when Zoe seems reluctant to talk.

"Really good," she smiles up at him brightly, then falters when she sees him frown.

"That's good...I suppose...," Palmer tails off, not wanting to put a dampener on the conversation so soon.

When they reach the beach there are lots of tourists already setting up for a day of sunbathing and sandcastle building.

The sun is warm, the sky is blue and cloudless, and the

sea is blissfully rolling back and forth with the tide.

"Why did you come," Zoe asks suddenly, not able to contain the question any longer. "You know why I came back here, you being here just negates all my efforts to get over you!"

"There's your answer, right there," Palmer stops, and turning holds on to both her hands. "I don't want you to get over me. I love you, Zoe. And right now I believe you love me – we need to fight to save what's ours, damn it!"

"What's ours...?" Zoe frowns up at him, confused.

With a dismissive shake of his head, Palmer says, "Just something Tara said. But you just need to know that I'm not going away. I'm going to fight to save our relationship even if you don't want me to!"

But Zoe had stopped listening around about the time he'd said... "Just something Tara said? When have you spoken to Tara?"

Realising his mistake, Palmer swallows hard then lifts his chin defiantly. "I arrived last night and had to speak to someone. I've only ever been to Tara's house, the day I came to fetch you when...when... Well that doesn't matter," he deviates, not wanting to remember the last time he'd been in Looe. "The fact is, Tara was my only contact so I called in last night before I booked into a hotel."

Now it was all beginning to make some kind of sense. "That's why she all but chased me out of the shop just now!" And pulling her hands away from his she stabs an accusatory finger repeatedly into his chest. "You talked her round. You sweet talked her into believing that you're my knight in shining armour when we both know that just isn't true!"

Now Palmer is frowning as deeply as Zoe as he catches her hand to stop her nails from jabbing into him.

"Right, because I'm some philandering villain that made love to you one minute then went off to have sex with some mystery woman the next," he shouts, then turns to glare at anyone brave enough to look over at them.

"Will you stop showing me up," she rages quietly. "I have to live here after you've done washing our dirty linen in public!"

"Fine! It's either here or your place – take your pick," he adds when her jaw drops for the second time that morning.

"You can't bully me-"

"Right, here it is then," Palmer continues as if Zoe hasn't spoken, but stops when her bottom lip begins to tremble.

"We need to talk, Zoe," he points out more

reasonably. "Surely you can see that."

Biting down on her bottom lip, Zoe simply nods wordlessly and begins to walk back in the direction of the town.

Not another word passed between them until they entered Zoe's cottage.

"Take a seat, if you want, I won't be a minute." Going up the steep stairs to her bedroom, Zoe fishes at the bottom of a drawer and pulls out the photos that had been sent by the anonymous note writer on her wedding day.

A minute later she was holding them out to Palmer, her face devoid of emotion, her hand steady though it longed to tremble.

Stupidly, Palmer hesitates to take them. He's wanted to get a look them from day one, yet now he is reluctant to see what Zoe had thought him capable of.

Now it is his turn to have his jaw drop in disbelief. "This is crazy," he exclaims, jumping to his feet and pacing the small living room. "That's me, but...it can't be...that never happened!"

His free hand is pushing back through his hair causing it to tumble and fall haphazardly.

Turning the photos over he sees the date and time stamp and still can't believe his eyes.

"Zoe, I promise you, this never happened – I've never seen that woman before in my life," he declares, imploring her to believe him.

And Zoe does find herself wavering.

If he's acting he's damned good. He really looks upset and frantic...but how can he be telling the truth when he's already admitted it's him in the photo? None of this makes sense!

"Just listen to what you're saying," Zoe tries to reason. "You've just admitted that is you in the photo, then you tell me that that little scene never happened – you can't have it both ways, Palmer. Either that is you or it isn't?!"

Continuing to frown and shake his head, even Palmer has a job understanding the situation.

"I know it sounds like I'm contradicting myself, but I don't know what else to say. I never kissed that woman – I don't care what these damned photos appear to show," he states adamantly, then angrily throws them into the empty fire grate.

"No!" Zoe dashes forward and reclaims them.

"Why the hell would you want to keep them," Palmer demands when she tucks them away in a drawer.

"To remind me why I'm here," she whispers, her voice beginning to tremble as she turns away from him.

Stepping behind her, Palmer holds his hands up to

place them on her shoulders to comfort her, but he hesitates then drops them to his side.

When she gets her threatening tears under control, Zoe turns to Palmer but he is no longer there.

"Palmer...?" But moving to the window, she watches Palmer striding down the path then down the street.

I'm sorry, Palmer...I just can't trust your love. I want to...but I can't.

All the way back to Birmingham, Palmer has to fight the urge to turn around and drag Zoe back to Birmingham with him.

He's seen the photos with his own eyes now, and even he doesn't know what to make of them.

It wasn't just somebody like me, it was me! But damn it, it wasn't. I never cheated on Zoe. I never kissed that damned woman!

But on reaching his home and parking the car, Palmer's troubles are about to get a lot worse.

Two men in suits step out of a nearby car and walk towards him.

"Mr Johnson?" one of them asks sternly.

With a frown, Palmer asks, "Who wants to know?"

"We'd like you to accompany us to the station, sir," the second suit says while holding his police badge out for Palmer's inspection.

"Is this about Connor – have you found something new?" He looks from one man to the other but sees nothing in either poker face.

"We have some questions for you that would be better asked at the station," was all the reply he got.

It doesn't occur to Palmer that this is anything other than a follow up on Connor's death. No one has been back to him about the body that had been found at his works, not since his initial interview.

"Take a seat, Mr Johnson," a more familiar voice tells Palmer.

It is the detective who first interviewed Palmer about Hickey's death, and now the penny begins to drop.

"This isn't about Connor at all, is it," he turns to look at the two men who'd brought him in before they turned to leave the room.

"Actually, it is...in part," the detective tells him as he takes a seat opposite Palmer.

Remaining quiet, Palmer waits to see where this is leading.

The second detective enters the room, again from his first interview.

"You remember Detective Cartwright?" the man sat opposite Palmer asks and gestures towards the man who gives Palmer a silent nod of his head. "And, in case you've forgotten, I'm Detective Carter. So let's get on with this, shall we?"

Palmer just stares across the table, he's good at playing poker too, and knows better than to shoot off his mouth before knowing exactly what is going on.

"Right! Hickey! We've been informed that you threatened his life even before your brother's death," Carter tells him, and Palmer narrows his eyes. "Don't you want to deny it?"

But Palmer just shakes his head; he had threatened Hickey that if he came anywhere near his brother again he would knock seven bells out of him.

"So you're admitting it?"

"Why am I here?" Palmer asks instead of answering.

"You're here because you threatened a man's life and now that man is dead," Cartwright tells him in a deadpan voice.

Carter nods in agreement and waits for Palmer's response, but he doesn't get one.

With an annoyed frown, Carter tells him, "If you think the silent tack is going to save you, you better think again!"

"Really. And why is that?"

"Because we've got a witness to your threat, smart arse!" Cartwright tells him, pushing off the wall he is leaning against.

"I'm not denying the threat, so now what," Palmer asks calmly.

Carter can't remember the last murder suspect he'd interrogated that had managed to stay as calm as this. "You're a cool customer, I'll give you that. But we're on to you. Take a look at this," Carter smiles and presses the button on a remote to bring the TV at the far end of the room to life, then activates a recording.

Palmer watches a very poor quality CCTV recording of him and Craig squaring up to Hickey outside of Jennings' place.

"And your point is...?"

"Don't get smart!" Cartwright snaps angrily. "It's clear from that footage that you were angry with Hickey about something. Maybe angry enough to kill him!"

But Palmer can't help a low chuckle. "Let me guess, when you questioned Jennings he 'offered' that piece of convenient evidence to lay the blame at my door." Palmer slowly shakes his head. "I didn't kill Hickey, though I might have given him a kicking before turning him over to you for Connor's murder. But in the circumstances, I think I would have been entitled to some payback – right?"

"Is that what happened," Carter asks quietly. "Did you give him a kicking that got out of hand?"

Looking directly into the detectives eyes, Palmer

doesn't hesitate. "No, I'm afraid I didn't get that pleasure." Then he stands and walks towards the door.

"Sit down!" Cartwright demands angrily.

"I don't think so," Palmer tells him calmly. "You have nothing, and you know it. And there's a reason for that," he tells them, looking from one man to the other, "I didn't murder Hickey – Jennings did!"

With that he leaves the room, and when Cartwright makes to follow him, Carter puts up a restraining hand.

"Leave him!" Giving a heavy sigh, Carter look up to where Cartwright is towering over him. "For what it's worth, I believe him. No one is that cool after committing murder, even accidentally."

"So we're back to Jennings?"

"I think he's right about that too – Jennings is our man, we just have to prove it!"

Driving straight over to Carly's house in search of Craig, Palmer pulls up on the front and climbs out of his car.

The big man's here alright. If this gets any more serious he'll be hearing wedding bells!

Jesus! My best friend will be married to my prospective mother-in-law. How weird is that?!

Before he can knock the door, Carly opens it and greets him with a warm smile.

"Palmer, good to see you, come on in," and she stands back to open the door wider. "Craig's out back. I only saw you because I came in for a cold drink and noticed your car pull up. Is everything ok?"

"Yes, no worries, Carly."

"That's not what Craig tells me," she informs him while showing Palmer out to the back patio. "I hear there's been some trouble down on the Dersinger building site."

They had both just stepped onto the patio and Craig gives her a warning frown.

"No problem," Palmer tells his friend. "Carly's family, but I'd rather word doesn't get around," he warns turning back to Carly.

"No, of course not," Carly assures him quickly.

"So what is the problem," Craig asks in a low rumbling voice. "Don't tell me you just came for a visit – though you're more than welcome any time."

Smiling broadly, Palmer nods and tells them, "You got me. I just came from the police station. Jennings has given them some CCTV of us outside his place talking with Hickey – only it doesn't look very friendly."

"And they think it shows your intention to murder him?" Craig frowns deeply. "Are they stupid or what? Jennings is obviously trying to distract them by pointing the finger at you. I wonder why they haven't questioned me yet – I was in that video too, I take it?"

"Oh yes – all big and bad looking," Palmer grins, then pulls it in when Carly gasps. "He was my wingman, that's all," he assures her, but she still looks concerned. "He wouldn't harm a fly."

"I know that as well as you do," Carly tells him indignantly. "I'm more concerned that you put Craig in danger. This man Jennings sounds very dangerous to me, not someone to be toyed with!"

"I'd like to say you're wrong, but I'd be lying," Palmer grimaces then turns to Craig. "I'm not too worried about the police, at least one of them seemed to have some sense about him. Though the other one..."

"Don't underestimate anyone," Craig tells him wisely. "Until Jennings is arrested you need to be concerned. If the police can hang this on you they will!"

"Hmm, maybe you're right," Palmer concedes. "Anyway, I just got back from a visit with Zoe..."

"You did! Is she alright? Is the baby alright?"

"They both appear to be fine," Palmer smiles, though less than enthusiastically.

"You don't look happy about somethin'," Craig tells him. "What happened?"

For a moment, Palmer looks down at his hands and

takes a deep breath. When he slowly exhales he looks from Carly to Craig then tells them, "I saw the photos. The one's that caused Zoe to leave me."

Carly's brows fly up, but it's Craig that asks, "And...?"

"And I don't know," Palmer admits. "It's me – as sure as I'm sitting here, the man kissing a woman I've never met in my life, is me. But I never did," he turns to Carly, imploring her to believe him.

She nods and her brows knit, "Did you bring them back with you?"

But Palmer shakes his head and lets out another sigh. "I was so damned angry I through them in the fire grate..."

"You did!" Carly gasps.

"It was empty," Palmer clarifies, then looks extremely annoyed. "Zoe rescued them and stuffed them in a drawer, and when I asked her why she kept them, she said 'to remind me why I'm here'. Just like that. She obviously believed the photos rather than me. So I left."

"Well it's difficult to argue with the evidence," Carly states in defence of her daughter. But adds, "Not that I'm saying I don't believe you. It's possible to alter anything these days I'm sure. Just look at the frauds people commit and get away with!"

Palmer sits back in his chair with a thump and smacks his forehead with his palm.

"What an idiot! I should have brought them with me and got them tested. Though I have to admit, they're good. If I didn't know it never happened, I'd believe I was having an affair."

"So you don't think Zoe will come home while she believes that the photos are real," Carly states rather than asks.

With a sad shake of his head, Palmer confirms her worst fears.

CHAPTER FOUR

Jennings was furious. *What do I have to do, spoon feed the damned cops!*

"Are you sure he walked out under his own steam?" he asks one of the men he'd told to follow the detectives that had paid him a recent visit.

"Yes sir, Mr Jennings, sir," the gormless goon confirms. "I saw them take him inside and then an hour later he comes walking out again, all by himself."

Closing his eyes in despair, Jennings takes a calming breath and steadies himself.

They don't have anything on me, not really. All they know is that Hickey worked for me...a bit of fetching and carrying, that's what I told them. And it looked like they swallowed it, especially when I mentioned Connor's brother and the tape.

One look at that and they'd been eager to have words with him. Yet they only kept him an hour. They kept me three, the idiots!

"Get back there and tell me what those keystone cops are up to. And next time, you phone me with any info. I don't want you letting them out of your site until they clock off duty. Is that clear," he glares up at the two men.

Both nodding and backing out of the room, they leave to do Jennings' bidding.

Jesus! I never thought I'd miss that trumped up fool, Hickey. But even he was preferable to the dunderheads I've been forced to use.

I'm gonna have to keep my eye out for some fresh talent. That guy I bribed at the Dersinger site seemed pretty keen to earn some extra cash once I made him an offer he couldn't refuse. Now that I've got him in my pocket I should be able to recruit him into my organisation!

"Yes. Not a bad idea. He'd be my man on the inside," Jennings chuckles to himself. "And Palmer would be none the wiser. I'd be working right under his self-righteous nose!"

Back in his loft flat, Palmer is once again studying his white board for more clues.

I'm positive now that Connor was selling me out to

Snelson. But how did that get him killed. If it was Hickey that beat the crap out of him, then why did he do it?

He must have thought he was doing Jennings a favour; he wouldn't have dared do it otherwise.

But where was the benefit to Jennings? What had Connor done to piss him off? I know he wasn't in debt to him – he was loaded when he died.

So where did all that money come from? I know Snelson paid him, but Snelson was all but washed up before Connor started selling me out.

This just keeps going round and round. None of it makes any real sense. And what about the notes to Zoe – Snelson wouldn't have had a hand in that!

Palmer stands back from the board and takes a good sip of whiskey. The fire water burns in his blood and then...

No! He wouldn't! He wasn't even here!

God damn it, Connor! Did you involve Laura in this, is that how the letters got on Zoe's car and to her mother's home?

If I thought for one minute...

But he doesn't let his mind go any further with the traitorous thought.

Connor was many things, but he wouldn't have done that. He cared for Zoe in his own warped way. He wouldn't have frightened her half to death. He wouldn't!

But the thought is never far from the surface, no matter how Palmer tries to push it away.

Having heard from Craig that Sean was recovering from home, Palmer decides to pay his injured employee a visit.

He's surprised to arrive outside a run-down bungalow, though the garden is immaculate.

Someone obviously loves gardening, but the house could do with a lick of paint.

Knocking on the front door, Palmer looks around while waiting for someone to answer it.

I wonder why Sean lives in this neighbourhood. It's a bit rough for him, I'd have thought. And it's not like he doesn't earn good money – especially now that Craig has made him up to foreman.

"Can I help you...," a pretty young woman asks, and he turns back to give her his full attention.

"Yes, I hope so. I'm Palmer Johnson...I just wanted to make sure that Sean is alright," he smiles hesitantly.

"Oh. We didn't expect anyone would come to look in on him," she fusses, wiping her hands on her apron. "I was just cooking in the kitchen and the lounge isn't as tidy as it should be..." but having said all that, the flustered woman opens the door wider and waves Palmer inside.

"It's your boss," she announces as they walk into a lounge that Palmer thinks looks 'lived in'. "You didn't tell me to expect a visitor...now look at us...all upside down..."

"Please, your home is fine. I didn't mean to make you uncomfortable," Palmer tries to reassure the woman, then turns his attention to Sean. "How are you doing, Sean? Are you suffering with headaches or stress after what happened?"

But Sean sits up and shakes his head, then pales visibly, obviously regretting the move. "Nothing to worry about," he tells Palmer with a hand to his right temple. "It isn't so bad when I lay my head down."

"Then why are you sitting up, man?" Palmer demands with a scowl. "This was a bad idea..." Standing up, he hesitates, then watches as Sean's wife comes to stand next to her husband

A sound makes them all turn, and they watch a young girl steer an electric wheelchair into the room.

"Stacy," her mother smiles. "This is your dad's boss, he called in specially to see how he's doing. That was nice, wasn't it?"

The young girl tips her head to one side and looks up at the stranger curiously.

"So you didn't come to sack him?" she asks bluntly.

Palmer is genuinely shocked, then realises why

everyone has been so uncomfortable with his visit.

"No, I haven't!" he confirms with a lift of his brow as he turns to her father. "For god's sake, Sean, don't you know me better than that!"

"I didn't say you would..." Sean colours up and looks sheepish. "I just said as I was worried. I mean, I knocked the damned wall down," he states, just as bluntly as his daughter had.

"You didn't do anything of the kind..."

"But I saw it," Sean interrupts.

"Yes, the wall has had to come down. The damage was too much to simply repair. But none of that was your fault," Palmer frowns down at Sean as he has to lie down again.

"Please, let me make you a cup of tea," Sean's wife offers, now that the worry over her husband's job has been lifted.

As Palmer nods and retakes his seat, the young girl in the wheelchair moves further into the room.

"I'm Cassie," she tells Palmer, pulling her wheelchair to a stop just short of his toes, then gives him a cheeky grin.

"You're pretty good with that, aren't you," he tells her, returning her grin and giving a low chuckle.

"Gotta get my fun somehow," she tells him.

"So, was it an accident, illness or birth that put you in there," he asks just as bluntly as she had been with him earlier.

Cassie doesn't flinch, but grins even wider. "You're not like the others. They're too scared to talk to me let alone ask what's wrong!"

"You're just different, not an alien." Then his smile widens, "Actually, it would be pretty cool to meet an alien, but I suppose you'll do for today."

Laughing loudly, Cassie does a spin in her wheelchair that would have made Palmer dizzy.

When she comes to a stop near his feet again, she's grinning like a Cheshire cat.

"I was in an accident at school. Stupid really, I used to do gymnastics but I fell awkwardly and did something to my spine," then she lifts her hands and raps them on the side of the wheelchair. "Now I get to ride around in one of these. It's not so bad," she adds bravely, turning to smile at her dad.

When the tea arrives, Sean's wife introduces herself as Karen and says, "I'm sorry about before. We don't usually treat guests that way."

Shaking his head, Palmer dismisses her worries with a wave of his hand and takes a sip of his tea.

"What did they say at the hospital?" Palmer asks. "I've

heard from Craig, of course, but he wasn't in the room with you."

"They were a bit concerned about the risk of a concussion when they saw the head wound. But I told them, I never passed out at any time and I don't have any dizziness," he explains. "It's just the headaches that lay me up a bit," he frowns, then turns to look at his wife.

"I've told you to rest up. There's nothing to do around here that I can't handle," Karen tells him with a reassuring smile.

"You're on the sick for as long as you need, and with full pay," Palmer adds when Sean looks concerned. "I told you that at the time, why the hell would you think I might sack you?"

"I just thought, once you'd had time to assess the damage and the costs you might not want me back after all."

Finishing his tea, Palmer once again gets to his feet and moves to stand next to the settee where Sean is laying.

Holding his hand out to him, Palmer waits for Sean to take it then gives it a firm shake.

"There's no way I'm losing one of my best men. I want you back to work the minute you're properly fit," Palmer tells him.

On the drive back to his flat, Palmer has time to think about Sean and the situation his family is in.

I had no idea he had those kinds of problems. I thought I knew my men pretty well, but he's always talked about his daughter like she was just like any other girl. Not struggling to come to terms with being in a wheelchair!

And she is struggling with it, no matter the brave face she tries to put on. I wonder how long it's been since the accident.

She looks about 12, though she acts a lot older. She's trying to reassure her parents, instead of the other way around.

One brave little cookie!

<u>CHAPTER FIVE</u>

The shop has been busy even with the extra help that Donna provides.

"If you could manage a couple of extra hours today girls, I'd be really grateful," Tara tells them, brushing her hair back from her face.

"If I could phone my mum I'm sure it would be alright," Donna smiles brightly.

"I'm fine too," Zoe adds, nodding and enjoying the happy atmosphere.

She had been fearful for her job when she'd heard about Donna coming back to work in the shop. But everything had turned out more than fine – they were fast becoming good friends.

"You know, I could always help out with Sara if you want to work more hours," Zoe offers when Tara goes into the back room.

"You would?" Donna asks, both surprised and delighted. "At the minute I can only do mornings. But if you really think it's ok, I could do a full day now and then, when you feel up to having Sara."

"No problem," Zoe agrees happily. "She'll give me some practice for when this little one arrives."

"I'll just go and ring my mum to ask her about staying today – it should be ok," Donna says, taking out her mobile and stepping away from the counter to make the call.

Moments later she returns with a happy smile. "No problem. My mum's great with Sara, and I mentioned about your offer and she thinks it's a great idea."

"Well that's good. We'll talk to Tara and see what extra hours you can do and then work something out," Zoe assures the young woman.

"Money's been a bit tight since Sara arrived," Donna explains. "It has already made a huge difference me being able to do a few hours, so any extra is welcome."

"That sounds good all around," Zoe chuckles. "You get more money, Tara get's the extra work done and I get to practice at being a mummy with Sara."

"What's this...?" Tara frowns with a half smile. Then she listens with a raised brow. "Are you sure you will be able to cope?"

"No problem. I haven't had the sickness for a while now, and I'm feeling really good," Zoe tells them with some relief.

"Oh dear, did you get morning sickness really bad?" Donna grimaces sympathetically.

"I couldn't keep anything down no matter what time of day it was," Zoe confirms. "I don't know who thought to call it morning sickness – mine was 24/7 for a long time."

"But you're sure you're alright now?" Donna asks with concern.

"I'm fine. In fact I feel better than fine...I feel great!" Then Zoe laughs and the other two women join in with her high spirits.

Tara has been worried about Zoe after Palmer left so suddenly. She could see how his visit upset her and still feels somewhat guilty for her part in the subterfuge.

But Zoe seems to be perking up, so maybe the work is just what she needs. And Donna is turning into a nice friend for her. The two might do each other a lot of good.

On Thursday of that week, Zoe looks after Sara for the first time.

"Oh wow, there's so much stuff," Zoe tells Donna wide eyed as she brings in a carry cot and then a bag filled with nappies and a whole host of things for the baby.

"Changing her nappy will be easy enough," Donna assures her. "Just do it like I showed you last night and you'll be fine. The disposables I use have a velcro type fastening that you can undo as many times as you like till you get it right.

"Are you really sure you want to do this?" Donna asks eyeing Zoe doubtfully. "It isn't too late for me to take her to my mother's."

"No, absolutely not!" Zoe tells her adamantly. "I'll be fine. Once I've done one I'll be well away, trust me."

"I've written everything down," Donna tells Zoe, showing her a list of instructions. "All her bottles are made up and she doesn't need them warmed up, I give them straight from the fridge and she's fine with that."

"Ok. And these are her nap times," Zoe points to the list.

"Yes. I try to have a little play with her in between times, just some silly play with her rattles and things — they're all in there," Donna tells her, indicating the bulging bag.

"Okee dokee," Zoe smiles, looking in on the sleeping baby laying in the carrycot.

"I'll call and make sure everything is going alright," Donna assures her. "And if you're at all unsure, my mobile number is at the top of the list I gave you."

"I'm sure everything will be fine," Zoe tries to sound confident. "Sara and I will be best friends by the time you come back. Now get off to work or you'll be late – then I'll be in trouble with Tara for holding you up."

Deciding to leave the carrycot where Donna had left it on the settee, Zoe gets a book to wedge under the side of it to make sure it can't tip if the baby turns over.

I'll move it to the dining table when she wakes up. I'm sure she's fine, but I'd feel better if she were on a solid surface.

Looking at the list, Zoe finds that she has a couple of hours till Sara's first feed.

Well you look peaceful enough. Ahh, a thumb-sucker. You are so cute...just look at your pretty button nose, and you have a lovely dimple in your chin.

I wonder what Brook will look like? Will she be like me or Palmer – I hope she has some of us both, but we'll just have to wait and see.

Less than an hour goes by before Donna is on the phone to see how she's getting on.

"Did she wake up after I left? I can't hear her grizzling but if she does she likes her hair tickled...it just seems to calm her," Donna adds with a smile in her voice.

"Donna, Sara is fine...she's still sleeping and looks very content," Zoe assures the baby's worried mum. "I've got my list and your contact number, but call any time if you're worried. Ok?"

"Ok," Donna sighs with relief. "I suppose I'm just being silly, but I've only ever left her with my mum and she's great with her."

"I'm really looking forward to giving Sara her first bottle," Zoe enthuses. "This is as much a benefit to me as it is to you, you know."

"Just don't forget, I have my mobile with me all the time if you have any problems. Ok?"

Standing at the kitchen sink a couple of minutes later, Zoe feels Brook give a flurry of kicks.

"Wow, baby. Did you just turn over or what?" With a hand to her swollen stomach, Zoe smiles with pride. Her baby feels so strong and she is looking forward so much to meeting her. Looking back in the living room, she rubs a hand gently over her restless baby.

"It won't be long now. Just another 16 weeks and you'll be in mummy's arms," she whispers, her love for her unborn child flowing through every word.

I wonder if Palmer counts down the weeks. It's obvious he knows the baby is his, but does he really care? Or will he walk away like he did from his other baby?

Frowning to herself, Zoe wonders about that snippet of information from the notes that had plagued her.

I would never have believed that of Palmer, he's always been so loving. But he cheated on me, so I suppose that makes me a poor judge of character anyway.

But even that doesn't feel right. And Palmer's reaction to the photos was pretty convincing. Could I really be that wrong about him? Could he be that good of an actor as to convince me to fall in love with him so deeply?

Distracted from her thoughts by the baby stirring, Zoe walks back into the living room and picks her up out of the carrycot.

"Hello, Sara," Zoe croons softly while holding the baby close to her chest. "Would you like your bottle? Mummy left it all ready for you, sweetie."

Going to the fridge, Zoe takes out the bottle and frowns. It feels very cold, but Donna had assured her that Sara was happy having it straight from the fridge.

"Ok, let's get comfy on the settee," she tells the baby, who is looking wide eyed back at her. "That's right, there you go."

"Well I'll be blowed...," Zoe smiles down at the baby in her arms, "...you really do like it!"

Grinning, she enjoys her first experience of feeding the baby. She'd visited with Donna the night before so that Sara would know her, and she'd held her for a while.

Having arrived too late to feed Sara, she had watched

Donna change her nappy but hadn't yet tried it out for herself.

Well, that's something we'll have to learn together, just you and me, Sara.

The ante-natal classes that Zoe has been attending have really paid off. She isn't as nervous as she thought she'd be, looking after Sara.

"But then, you are such a good girl," she smiles down at the baby lying on the changing mat. "And now you're all nice and clean again too."

I think I'm going to use disposable nappies too. They are so easy and convenient!

The next day, Zoe goes to work feeling really pleased with herself and can't wait to tell Tara all about looking after Sara.

"I swear she smiled at me," Zoe states happily. "She's a little angel, and good as gold."

Tara chuckles at her zeal. "Just wait till your own arrives – then we'll see if all this enthusiasm lasts!"

"I know it won't be all sweetness and light," Zoe admits reproachfully. "But I'm so looking forward to holding Brook in my arms – surely nothing can be so bad as to overshadow that!"

"Hmm," is all Tara elects to say, deciding not to rain on Zoe's parade just now.

"Well I can't wait," Zoe declares again with a hand lovingly caressing her stomach.

"So you think you'll be happy to mind her again?" Tara asks curiously.

"Oh yes! Of course! And Donna seems happy with the arrangement," Zoe tells her with a huge smile.

"And I'm certainly happy with the extra help," Tara confirms. "We got some more orders in yesterday so there will be plenty to do."

By teatime, Zoe is ready to go home. She has to admit, if only to herself, it is getting more difficult to work a long day.

Perhaps I should consider going back to doing just 3 mornings a week. Especially if Donna wants to work the extra hours.

After saying 'bye' to Tara, Zoe steps out of the shop and into the summer heat.

Talk about 'flaming June', this heat-wave is a killer!

"You look a bit pale – are you sure you're not doing too much?"

Zoe spins around to see who is talking to her and comes face to face with Palmer.

Gasping in shock, she puts a hand to her racing heart and has to try and steady herself.

Before she knows it, Palmer has her in his arms,

holding her to him and looking down at her with avid concern.

"What are you doing here?" she gasps when her breathing comes under control.

"I told you last week, I'm not going away," he states firmly. "I'm going to love you until you finally believe I'm sincere."

"But I don't want you here," she tells him stubbornly, wrenching herself out of his arms.

"Tough! I'm not giving up, you mean too much to me for that," he tells her with a smile that tilts her heart.

"Palmer, please," she begs imploringly. "I can't do this. Are you deliberately trying to upset me?"

Shaking his head calmly, Palmer looks her straight in the eyes and his smile slips. "No. But I won't let you continue to believe the worst of me either. I've never done anything to deserve your contempt. Until I can convince you of that, I'll be around," he tells her flatly.

CHAPTER SIX

"You can't do this," she tells him desperately. "You can't force me to see you if I don't want to."

Walking as quickly as she can under the circumstances, Zoe tries to leave Palmer behind.

"That's where you're wrong," he grins impishly. "I'll be around until you see sense. I have never, nor would I ever, cheat on you Zoe Benson. And before I'm done, you'll believe that!"

Continuing to walk rapidly, Zoe tries to get away from Palmer but he easily keeps up.

Before long they reach the cottage and Zoe walks up to her front door then turns to glare at Palmer.

"You are not coming in!" she states defiantly, glaring hotly and lifting her chin.

"Fine," Palmer smiles annoyingly. "I'll just sit out here and wait."

With that he walks to the end of the short path and parks himself on the low wall, then looks back at Zoe with his arms folded resolutely.

"Oh! You're impossible!"

Getting out her key, Zoe lets herself into the cottage and slams the door behind her.

Palmer chuckles deeply, loving her spirit and hoping that Zoe will eventually take pity on him.

Less than five minutes pass when she comes to the front door, opens it then turns her back on him.

He finds her in the kitchen, filling a kettle and bristling with annoyance.

"I knew you wouldn't leave me out there to fry in the sun," he tells her.

"Don't bet on it," she glares at him before plugging the kettle back in.

"You know you love me," Palmer teases, his smile tugging at Zoe's tender heart.

"I've never denied that," she surprises him by saying. "I just can't trust you anymore!"

His smile gone, Palmer takes a seat at the breakfast table and considers his next words very carefully.

"Think about it, Zoe. Think about us and the amount of time we spent together," he tells her more seriously. "When, exactly, did I have time to meet and cavort with another woman?"

Hesitating, Zoe looks at him intently.

"I want to believe you," she says eventually. "But even you admitted that it is you in those photos. So how can you sit there and deny being unfaithful to me?"

Heaving a heavy sigh, Palmer nods in confirmation. "I can't deny that I am in those photos. But how, I honestly can't say."

Putting a hand to her forehead, Zoe tries to stop her world from spinning.

"You can't do this...you really can't!"

"I want to take them back with me," he tells her, though she doesn't appear to hear him. "Zoe...I want to get the photos tested."

"Tested...?"

"Yes. I want to get the photos tested to verify that they are fakes."

Staring at him blankly, Zoe slowly shakes her head. "You can't have them, they're mine."

With raised brows, Palmer regards her carefully. "Why on earth would you want to hang on to something so hurtful? I really don't understand you're obsession with them. It's like you're willing them to be real!"

Growing angry, Zoe stands with hands on hips glaring at Palmer. "You've got some cheek coming all the way down here just to pick a fight! I didn't invite you. In fact, you should go. Right now, you should go and never come back."

Feeling amazingly calm, Palmer just stares her down and shakes his head.

"I'm here for a weekend break, so I'll be around for the next couple of days."

"Well you're not staying here!"

"Nope. I'm staying at the same hotel where I stayed the last time I was here," his smile annoyingly smug.

"Oh!"

His smile spreading across his face as Palmer realises he's stolen her thunder; he gets up and takes her in his strong arms.

"There's no getting rid of me, Zoe Benson," he states firmly while looking into her heated brown eyes. "When I love, it's forever so it looks like you're stuck with me!"

Before she can utter another word, his lips are on hers and she isn't fighting him off.

I love you too, Palmer. I always have.

With his arms around her, with his scent in her nostrils and driving her wild, Zoe drinks of him like a woman with a thirst that can never be quenched. Until he pulls away...

"Get some rest," he tells her as he walks to the kitchen door and looks back. "I'll come and see you in the morning."

With that he is gone, and Zoe is left longing for him to come back.

This is so stupid! You can't expect him to leave you alone if you respond like a wanton sex starved woman the minute he holds you in his arms! Get a grip! He's just a man!

Then she smiles the smile of a woman that knows so much better.

No, he really isn't. Palmer has never been 'just' anything. He's so handsome, and he's built like a porn star. And you're even more in love with him now than you've ever been!

Stupid! Stupid! Stupid! You need to steer clear of Palmer Johnson. He is bad for your health and peace of mind!

But when she goes to bed a few hours later, it's Palmer she dreams of and the way his hands and lips can make her feel.

A hard knock at her front door has Zoe scurrying out of bed and dragging on a dressing gown before going to open it.

When she does, she finds Palmer smiling down at her in all his glorious perfection.

But Zoe is less than impressed.

"What the hell, Palmer? I thought you told me to rest

– then you come round here at some ungodly hour waking me up!"

Going through to the little kitchen, it's Palmer who puts the kettle on and gets the mugs down ready to make them some coffee.

"That just shows how right I am about you needing to take things a bit easier," he tells her, then watches her frown with confusion. "It's 9:30," he points out, smiling as sudden dawning spreads across her face.

"It can't be! I never sleep in that late," she states, before running into the lounge to check the time.

Pouring the boiling water into the mugs, Palmer chuckles when he hears her groan.

"Come on, sleepy head, I've made you a nice cup of coffee to wake you up," he grins.

"Jesus! I feel sort of hung over," Zoe admits, taking a seat opposite Palmer at her breakfast table.

"I want you to promise me you'll cut down your hours at the shop," he tells her softly.

"But I love my work," she raises her chin stubbornly, even though she has been thinking along the same lines herself.

"It isn't just you you have to think about now though, is it?"

She knows he's right, but he's already been right once

today and she isn't in the mood to prove him right twice.

"Me and the baby are doing just fine," she tells him stiffly.

"I'm sure you are...for now," he adds ominously. "But how would you feel if that changed because you aren't taking care of yourself?"

With her jaw dropping open, Zoe stares at Palmer like he's accused her of murder.

"I would never do anything to put Brook in danger," she gasps.

"Not deliberately, I'll grant you. But being stubborn just for the sake of going against me is idiotic and wrong," he tells her bluntly.

Her ramrod straight spine finally slumps as she admits that he's right. "I was already thinking about cutting my hours back now that Donna is working at the shop," she concedes ungraciously. "You just got me wound up the way you demand things – like you've got a right to tell me what to do!"

"Don't I have a right to say when I'm worried that you're not looking after yourself, and therefore putting our daughter at risk?"

There, it was out in the open. Finally the truth was to be spoken between them.

"I didn't say that Brook was yours," she murmurs, her eyes lowered to study her drink.

"But we both know that she is," he tells her just as softly.

Nodding silently, Zoe can't stop the tears from falling. "I never meant to hide her from you. I didn't even know I was pregnant when I came here. It was Tara who realised what was wrong when I started to feel ill all the time."

"That must have been pretty scary for you," Palmer tells her. "But didn't you think I had a right to know when you came back to Birmingham for Connor?"

"But she was his by then," Zoe cries desperately. "He was so happy when we found out that she was a girl, and he gave her her name. He was so proud and looking forward to being a daddy."

"But she was never really his," Palmer states, trying to hold all the hurt inside. "Would you have allowed her to grow up thinking that my brother was her father?"

Looking up, Zoe can see the hurt that Palmer is unable to hide completely.

"It wasn't like that," she tells him, reaching a hand across the table to lay over his. "You already have a child that you don't even see, so why would you want to be saddled with mine?"

"So that's it," Palmer snatches his hand away. "We're back to the notes and the fact that you're all too willing to believe every word they say!"

Getting up, Palmer paces the small room his hands pushing back through his hair in frustration.

"Why is it so much easier to believe that crap when I'm right here telling you that none of it is true," he demands bitterly.

"I don't know..."

"Well I do! It comes back to those damned photos," he states, coming to a stop right in front of her. "You were fine until they arrived – I want the chance to prove my innocence. I want those photos, Zoe, and I'm not leaving without them!"

Hesitating, Zoe contemplates her hands.

"Zoe!"

"Alright! Ok! You can have the damned photos," she tells him, pushing past him to get them. "There...," she snaps angrily, "...are you satisfied?!"

Nodding, he puts the photos safely in his wallet then puts his hands on her shoulders.

"I just want the chance to prove to you that I'm telling the truth? Even a murderer gets his day in court," Palmer reasons quietly.

"I suppose," she concedes, and actually feels lighter now that the issue has been settled. "How do you fancy a walk on the beach? I need some fresh air."

Smiling brightly, grateful for the change of mood, Palmer nods in agreement.

"You go shower and get dressed and I'll make you some breakfast," he tells her. "Then we'll go for that walk."

The sky is now overcast and the sea looks grey while they walk hand in hand along its edge.

"I can see why you like it here," Palmer tells her with a contented smile. "It really is beautiful and your cottage reminds me of the one we stayed in when we got engaged."

Tilting her head to look up at him, Zoe is pleased to see that he looks happy in recalling that memory.

"I thought that too, the moment I saw it," she admits. "We were so happy back then."

Deciding not to push his luck, Palmer lets her dwell on that fact and bends to collect a few shells from the sand.

"I'll bet you could make something pretty with these," he smiles, holding them out to her in his large palm.

"They are lovely. So delicate," she muses, touching them with a gentle finger. "Let's look for more, then I can really have a go at making something nice."

For the next couple of hours they enjoy each other's company and the simple pursuit of seashell hunting.

By lunch time, Zoe is feeling more happy and relaxed than she has in a long time.

"We've got lots," she smiles brightly, examining their cache.

"That should keep you busy for a bit on your days off," Palmer tells her, hinting at her need to reduce her hours of work.

"Ok," she concedes without a fight. "I know it makes sense, I'll tell Tara on Monday. I'm sure she won't mind now that Donna is back."

Buying a small bag to stow the seashells in, Palmer and Zoe go off to enjoy a midday meal together.

"Today has been great," Zoe admits when their meal is finished and the coffee arrives.

"I'm glad you've enjoyed yourself. You certainly look better than you did," he remarks, looking her over with concerned eyes. "I don't like seeing you look so tired and dejected."

She is about to deny his claim, but decides that honesty is the best policy after such a lovely day together.

"You're right," she nods, and doesn't pull her hand away when he reaches across the table to hold it. "It's been hard cutting myself off from my family, and especially from you."

"Then come back, Zoe," he pleads softly. "Even if you move back in with your mum, at least you wouldn't be so far away," he reasons, knowing how close the two women are.

With a long sigh, Zoe shakes her head. "It is tempting – but it just wouldn't be right."

Giving her hand a gentle squeeze, Palmer asks, "Why not? Your mum would love to help you through all this. She's missing you as much as I am, and I'm not exaggerating just to lay more guilt on you."

"No, I know. But it's taken me all this time to get settled down here," she explains. "I can't just give it all up on a whim."

"If that's what you want, I won't try to force you," he tells her, somewhat hurt to have his feelings written off as a 'whim'.

"Thank you. I really mean that. Thank you for not making this any harder than it already is," she smiles sadly, turning her hand upwards to wrap her fingers around his.

CHAPTER SEVEN

They'd had a great weekend after the rough start. Palmer even fancied that Zoe had wanted him to stay the night at the cottage after their chilled out evening with fish and chips and a bottle of wine.

Zoe had chosen the film; an old tearjerker called 'A Star Is Born' staring Barbra Streisand and Kris Kristofferson. And he'd enjoyed wrapping his arms around her when she'd cried at 'John-Norman's' death.

But she had definitely seemed a little put out when he'd announced it was time to go and for her to get some sleep.

It brings a smile to his lips to think of it.

Maybe that's what I need to do...hold back and let her come to me! Maybe she'll want what she can't have – not that it'll be easy.

Having her so close was painful, yet not having her near me at all is draining the life-force out of me.

I can't exist without Zoe. I know that, why can't she feel it too?!

When he calls into his office, Palmer finds the door closed and the two secretaries looking worried.

"Who's in there?" he asks, jerking a thumb towards his office door.

Mandy turns sharply, startled by his sudden appearance.

"It's Mr Stanley and Sean Derwent," Mandy informs him cautiously.

Not saying another word, Palmer strides over to his office door, opens it then closes it firmly behind him.

"What's going on," he asks, narrowing his eyes to assess the situation.

Sean jumps to his feet and shifts them uncomfortably while studying his hands.

"Wanted to talk to you and Craig," he mutters, still not meeting Palmer's eyes.

So Palmer turns to Craig, "What's this all about?"

"I think I should let Sean explain," Craig sighs deeply, a large hand wiping over his distressed face.

"Sean...?" That was all Palmer had to say for Sean to lift his head and stare him straight in the eyes. "You got something you want to say to me?"

Nodding sadly, he says, "Yes boss, I do."

"Then retake your seat and get on with it man," he demands bruskly, wanting Sean to spit out whatever it is that's causing him such discomfort.

"It's about the accident, boss," he begins uncertainly. "It was my fault. I didn't know that's what was going to happen, but it was my fault anyway," he tails off, and his eyes drop to study his hands again.

Looking at Craig for an explanation, the big man just lifts his hands palms upwards, then says, "Sean seems to think he owes you this," and he tosses a fat A5 envelope across the desk to Palmer.

When he opens it, Palmer's frown deepens as he looks back at his friend.

"What the hell is this?"

"It's the money I was paid for leaving the tool shed unlocked," Sean's quiet voice penetrates Palmer's confused thoughts.

"You did what...?!"

"I thought he was just going to lift some of the gear – slow you up a bit and disrupt the job," Sean pleads, the guilt of what could have happened eating away at him. "But when I heard about those drills being cross wired and how they could have killed a man if he'd used them...well...I couldn't stay quiet. Especially not after your visit to the house. Me and Karen agreed; what I'd done was wrong and you deserve better than that."

Craig's brows are almost in his hairline, but Palmer has gone still and cold.

"You sold me out to someone who you thought wanted to rip off my tools..."

It is said so quietly, so matter of fact, that Sean has to look up to see Palmer's expression.

"I'm sorry, boss. When he phoned me at home, I knew I had to come and tell you everything," Sean explains. "You see, he wants me to do something else...something more."

Feeling nothing but contempt and bitter disappointment in his judgment, Palmer rounds the desk to stand next to Craig and lean against the back wall.

"And what exactly does this person want you to do?" Palmer asks, his hardened blue eyes piercing into Sean's.

"I.I don't know, boss," Sean admits. "He said he'd get back to me when the time was right. Only, he told me that if I tell you anything about it my family would pay."

Craig pulls in a sharp breath and looks up at Palmer. "Sounds like someone we know," he growls, his gravel edged voice now deep with disdain.

"Jennings!"

"Yep!" Leaning back in his seat, Craig turns to look up at Palmer. "What are you thinking?" Craig asks, remembering how Palmer had wanted to go sort Jennings out on his own the last time.

"I'm thinking I want to go wring that mongrel's fat little neck!" Palmer replies scathingly.

Then he looks across at Sean and considers his options.

"But I'm not going to do anything...," he muses, his eyes boring into Sean, "...you are!"

"Me!" Sean gasps in surprise, but then he nods and takes a long breath to calm himself. "You're right, I need to put this right. I would never have let you down if he hadn't offered me so much damned money," Sean tells them, his calloused hands rubbing over his tired face. "I'm such a fool!"

"Why didn't you come to me if you needed money so damned bad?!" Palmer snaps, hurt by the betrayal of a man he'd trusted.

"It was for Cassie," he finally admits, ashamed of his actions. "Now I've made things a hundred times worse and she still won't get her operation."

"Operation...?" Craig frowns over at Sean.

"Yes, there's a chance that Cassie might walk again if we can get her over to a surgeon we found in America,"

Sean tells them flatly. "This money offer came right after we found him on the internet and got in touch. It seemed like a gift from the gods at the time, but I was kidding myself...I knew it was wrong. I'm sorry, boss," Sean lifts his head to look Palmer straight in the eyes to show his sincerity.

"Shit!" Palmer explodes, pushing himself away from the wall. "And you never at any time thought to come to me for help? What the hell is wrong with you?!"

"Sorry, boss," Sean repeats, hanging his head in shame.

"He did his homework," Craig interjects gruffly.

"Yes...," Palmer agrees while looking at Sean, "he certainly did."

"Who...?" Sean asks confused.

"Jennings!" Palmer spits out, like the man's name causes a bad taste in his mouth. "He didn't just pick you out of the bunch and say, 'he looks like a nice guy, go ask him to leave the tool shed unlocked!'"

"You think he knew about Cassie?" Sean asks in stunned disbelief. "But how?"

"A lowlife like Jennings has his ways," Craig tells him. "It's his bread and butter – find a man's weakness then move in for the kill. He wouldn't have thought twice about the men that could have been killed while he was trying to get back at Palmer!"

Paling visibly, Sean looks from Craig to Palmer and back again. "And this is the man you think threatened my family... Oh Christ, what have I done!"

Before they can discuss things any further, Palmer's mobile insistently demands his attention.

"Yes," he snaps, then reigns himself in and apologises. "Sorry, you caught me at a bad time. How can I help?"

He listens and his brow creases then he loses all colour and says, "I'm leaving right now. No, no, I'm on my way. But do me a favour...don't tell her I'm coming!"

"Palmer, what the hell...?" Craig demands when he makes to leave the room without saying a word.

"It's Zoe, I don't know the details but she's in the hospital," he tells them. "I'll be in touch the minute I know anything," he promises, then disappears before Craig can ask anything else.

After a tortuous journey, Palmer arrives at Derriford Hospital and has to spend an age driving around trying to find a parking spot.

By the time he finds Tara, having rung her from his mobile, Palmer is frantic.

"Just take a breath," Tara warns when Palmer comes rushing over to her looking fit to drop from a heart attack. "She's fine, she's fine," Tara repeats when Palmer doesn't appear to hear her.

"Then why is she here," Palmer demands.

"It turns out she's got some sort of urine infection that is particularly nasty," Tara explains. "It happens...," she states with a dismissive shrug, "...only Zoe ignored the fact that she wasn't feeling well until she broke into a fever." Looking dubiously at Palmer, Tara decides to tell him everything.

"I only found her because she was due in to work and didn't turn up. Which, as we both know, isn't like Zoe at all."

Any colour that Palmer had drains with the realisation of what could have happened.

"So, if this had happened tomorrow..."

"Exactly! I wouldn't have had any reason to check on her as she wouldn't have been working anyway."

Watching him pace back and forth with his hands pushing back through his hair in frustration, Tara waits for him to calm down.

"You know she needs to come home, right?" Palmer states rather than asks when he comes to an abrupt halt in front of her. "I mean, we both know it isn't safe for her to be alone. She doesn't know her nearest neighbours, so even they wouldn't be alerted if they didn't see her for a while!"

"Come on...," Tara encourages, walking ahead to show

the way, "...you'll drive yourself crazy with 'what ifs' when what really matters is that Zoe is ok and you need to see her."

Hauling in a steadying breath, Palmer releases it slowly.

"You're right, I know it. But I could give her a good spanking for putting us all through this!"

When Tara turns a sharp look on him, Palmer shakes his head with the beginnings of a smile tugging at his lips.

"Metaphorically speaking," he assures her. "Not that she doesn't deserve the other kind; as I'm sure her mother would agree if she knew what was going on."

"So you haven't told her," Tara asks as they step into the lift.

"I didn't get the chance, though I was with her partner when your call came through. I promised to call as soon as I know anything," he explains.

"Ok, this way," Tara tells him as they step off the lift and she begins to lead the way again.

"Did you mention anything to Zoe?"

"About you coming? No, you asked me not to," Tara frowns up at him.

"I know, but... Thanks," he smiles as they stop outside of the locked ward doors.

"No problem. Just don't go upsetting her or I might regret my decision!"

Having negotiated entry to the unit via the intercom, Palmer and Tara make their way to Zoe's room.

"Tara! Am I glad to see you…"

"Hello, Zoe," Palmer greets her with a concerned look that takes in the IV line going into her wrist.

"Palmer!" she gasps, looking from Tara to Palmer and then back again with an accusatory stare.

"Don't go blaming Tara," Palmer tells her, guessing correctly at the look exchanged between the two women. "I insisted on coming – what did you expect when you collapse at home on your own?!"

"I..you..what are you talking about," Zoe splutters desperately. "I'm fine! It's just a urine infection!"

"An infection that caused you to collapse with a fever," Palmer emphasises quietly.

Holding out a hand, Tara moves to intervene. "Ok, let's just calm down."

"I just wanted to see that you're alright – is that so wrong," Palmer demands, his quiet voice more worrying to Zoe than if he had shouted at her.

"No, I suppose not," she sulks with a frown.

"Good. Now tell me what that is going into your arm," he asks, pointing to a small plastic bag with a little clear fluid still in it.

"It's an antibiotic. They could have given it to me

orally but this way they can get it straight into my system and working quicker," she explains.

"So, you look much better than when I found you," Tara chimes in, somewhat relieved that the crisis has passed. "Have you managed to get any sleep?"

"Mmm," Zoe nods, rubbing her eyes with her knuckles. "I don't know why I'm still so tired. You'd think being passed out on the floor for...for a while would count as sleep," she stumbles, having realised just in time that she had been about to say all night.

Then what would Palmer have said! Jesus, this is like walking on eggshells!

But if she thinks Palmer hasn't noticed her near slip, she's wrong.

"So you didn't get any sleep last night," he asks curiously.

Being a very poor liar, Zoe's pale cheeks gain a sudden flush of colour.

"I just think, maybe, the fever has left me more tired than I realised," she evades deftly.

"So you didn't sleep well," Palmer persists.

"Will you just drop it! I've been sleeping loads today," Zoe insists adamantly, scowling at Palmer with a look that might kill the faint hearted.

But Palmer is made of sterner stuff, and decides to come right out with it.

"You were on the floor all night, weren't you," he demands, and watches Zoe's nervous hand clutch at the base of her throat. "For christ's sakes, Zoe, are you willing to risk our child's life for the sake of your wilful and stubborn independence?!"

Drawing in a startled breath, Zoe's mouth opens and closes like a guppy's, but not a word comes out.

"Sweetie, if that's true, maybe you should listen to Palmer. I lost a babe in the earlier stages, but even then the emotional pain of it has never left me," Tara whispers softly.

Reaching out a hand, Zoe takes Tara's in a show of support. "I'm so sorry, you never said."

With a grim smile, Tara says, "It isn't something I talk about. It was six years ago, but it might as well be yesterday for all the heartache it still brings."

"But, you're not blaming yourself, are you," Zoe asks, giving Tara's hand a gentle squeeze. "It happens to lots of women; I know, I've read about it in the magazines I bought."

Heaving a sigh, Tara shakes her head. "This time, I think it really was my fault." Then she holds up a hand when Zoe makes to protest. "I was working too hard, stocking up the shop and moving a lot of heavy gear. I didn't take enough care – don't let this be you in a year or two's time, telling someone how much you regret losing your child. It will never leave you, if it happens!"

With tear filled eyes and a trembling bottom lip, Zoe reaches out to offer Tara a hug.

When the two women break apart, Zoe turns to Palmer and asks, "Ok. So what do you suggest?"

"I suggest you let me take you home and look after you," he states, with more calm and restraint now that she is being reasonable.

"Home? With you?" Zoe asks with raised brows.

"With your mother, if that's what it takes to look after you," he sighs heavily.

But rather than agree right away, Zoe turns to Tara with concern in her eyes. "Won't you need me? You said you had a lot of new orders; I can't just leave you in the lurch!"

"I have Donna and a friend that doesn't mind helping out when I'm stuck," Tara smiles reassuringly. "I'll miss you, for sure, but you and the babe come first."

CHAPTER EIGHT

"I don't want anything to do with this," Henry Snelson tells Jennings when he enters the crook's office.

"So I hear," Jennings tilts his head to one side and considers the large man in front of him. "Yet you accepted my help to keep your company afloat. Don't you think I deserve some reciprocation for my trouble?"

"I'm paying you back," Snelson snaps angrily. "And a lot of interest besides."

"And you're an ungrateful son-of-a-bitch," Jennings accuses, his eyes narrowed and focusing on his nervous quarry.

"What is it you want," Snelson asks, taking a seat when the two men behind him push him towards it.

"I want you to start paying me back for the favour I did you," Jennings smiles slyly. "I want your help in bringing Palmer Johnson down to size!"

Spluttering helplessly, Snelson pales at the thought of what Jennings is asking him to do. "I won't kill anyone...I can't," he gasps and pants, his breath coming in short, panicked gulps.

"When did I mention the word 'kill'," Jennings sneers with a look of complete disgust. "I'm talking about ruining his reputation, forcing him out of business and costing him everything he owns!"

"But how, I don't know anything about that sort of thing," Snelson sits back in his seat with some relief. "You'd be far better at that than I would."

"But I don't have your contacts," Jennings lies, sitting back in his seat observing the poor excuse for a human being sat opposite him. "However, I do have other means at my disposal, and I will be utilising them to be sure."

Shifting in his seat, Snelson misinterprets Jennings' remark as a threat. "There's no need for that, I'll do it but it may take a little time," he concedes, sweat beading on his brow.

For a second, Jennings frowns then smiles when he realises what Snelson has assumed.

"Just don't let me down...," Jennings warns, playing up his part, "...or I'll have to consider my other options...won't I!"

Carly is on tenterhooks, waiting for Zoe to arrive. Palmer had told Craig what was going on so that when Zoe phoned her mother he would be clued in and able to support her.

"I thought they'd be here by now," Carly says again, pacing in front of the lounge window. "Didn't you say that Palmer told you they were leaving – that was 6 hours ago!"

Coming up alongside her, Craig draws her to a halt by putting his large arm round her shoulders.

"Woman, you are going to wear a hole in the floor if you keep this up," Craig smiles understandingly. "No doubt Palmer is taking his time as he has a pregnant lady for a passenger," he explains, and receives a grateful smile in return.

"That's right!" Carly explains. "I'll bet that's right, and I do want him to drive careful..."

"But you want your girl home too," he chuckles deeply.

"Oh! Oh! Oh! Here they are!" And before he can take his next breath, Craig watches Carly dash to the front door and she is off down the drive to greet them.

Palmer is out and rounding the car quickly to lend Zoe a hand. Her increased size makes it more difficult for her to alight his low slung car.

Before Zoe can take another step, Carly has her in a hug that tells her daughter just how worried she has been.

"It's ok, mum, I'm fine," Zoe tells her, returning the hug and glad to be home.

"No more of this living in Cornwall...," Carly tells her tearfully, "...my nerves just won't stand it.

"Hmm, you're not the only one demanding that I live up here," Zoe frowns over at Palmer.

"Then I'm glad to have you on side," Carly declares, then draws Zoe up to the house where Craig is waiting to greet her.

"How you doin', Princess," he asks with a grin. "Mind the hole in the floor near the window, you're mother wore it out waiting for you to get here!"

Carly tuts at him, but everyone else enjoys the joke and the atmosphere is soon relaxed and homey.

With a cup of tea in hand and her closest friends and family all concerned for her welfare, Zoe feels loved and happy.

"It really does feel great to be home," she tells them with a tear in her eyes. "I have missed everyone."

"I'll go and fetch your cases in," Palmer excuses himself so that Zoe can have some private time with her mother and Craig. But Zoe follows him out to the car.

"I was including you in that, you know," she tells Palmer shyly as he unlocks the boot and removes both her cases.

"That's good to know. But I won't hound you, Zoe. I wanted you back here to keep you and the baby safe...not to hound you into coming back to me," he states, leaving her standing while he hauls the cases up the drive and into the house.

Well! I try to hold out an olive branch and get smacked over the head with it! What the hell did I do wrong...I said I missed him, damn it!

But as she is walking back to the house, Palmer says goodbye to her mother and Craig then gives her a wave and takes off in his car.

"What the heck is wrong with Palmer," she asks, looking at Craig with a perturbed frown.

"Didn't notice anythin'," he tells her, his brows raised innocently. But he has his own ideas about what is going on.

"Ok. Well...I think I'm going to lie down on the bed for a bit. I'm shattered," Zoe adds with a yawn she can't stifle.

"Sounds like a good idea," her mother encourages with a smile. She is so pleased to have her daughter home and hopes to convince her to stay in Birmingham, if not the family home, even after the baby is born.

Feeling bereft for some inexplicable reason, Zoe lies on her bed but tosses and turns as her thoughts do the same.

What's his problem, I wasn't exactly coming on to him. He wishes!

But I did think he' be glad that I'd missed him. Thrilled even, if his professions of love are to be believed.

I mean, why travel all the way to Cornwall to convince me that he loves me then give me the cold shoulder once he gets his way and I come back here?

Damn it, Palmer Johnson!

Back in his flat, Palmer is puzzling over his whiteboard and adding bits of information.

Then a loud knock comes at his door and Palmer frowns, wondering who it can be.

"Mr Johnson...," a familiar voice greets him as he opens the door, "...we need to ask you a few more questions."

Heaving a sigh, Palmer opens the door wider, "Then you'd better come in. What can I help you with now," he frowns, annoyed at being pulled away from the whiteboard and the thoughts he'd been piecing together.

With a raised brow, Inspector Carter moves further into the room and looks a Palmer speculatively.

"Were you busy with something," he asks pointedly.

"Yes, but what do you want," Palmer asks, not moving from standing next to the front door.

"This is a nice place," the talkative inspector observes. "Very nice, and spacey too."

Walking as he talks, the inspector comes to a stop in front of the whiteboard.

"That's nothing to do with you!" Palmer crosses the room and tries to come between the inspector and all the information written on the display, but Cartwright holds him back.

"This is good work," Carter proclaims, nodding his head as he reads and digests the information. Then he points a finger at one of the names. "She did the notes to your girlfriend," he states with a surety that comes from years of doing the job. "Have you spoken to her yet?"

Palmer stops his efforts to extricate himself from the restraining grip of Inspector Cartwright and looks at Carter as if he's gone mad.

"Are you crazy," he frowns deeply. "You know nothing about her yet you finger her in a matter of seconds – am I supposed to be impressed?"

"Not really – I'm just pointing out the obvious," Carter smiles, turning to Palmer with a curious look in his eyes. "Yet I get the feeling you disagree – why?"

Shucking his way free of Cartwright, Palmer moves to

stand next to Carter and they both contemplate the board.

Damn it, Connor, it's a good job you're dead or your arse would be in the wind right now!

"We've pretty much worked out that Connor was selling me out to Snelson and that Laura must have lent him her keys to get into the office," Palmer admits reluctantly. "But as for the notes...," he shakes his head, "...she wouldn't have done that. Laura and Zoe were tight. They went out together and confided in each other – she wouldn't have done that."

"Hmm, from an insider's point of view I can see where you're coming from," the inspector nods. "But from an objective point of view I'm telling you she's the one!"

"Why would you even think that? Laura has worked for me reliably and honestly for years. The only crazy thing she did was fall in love with my brother!"

"Exactly!" Carter exclaims firmly. "Love trumps friendship every time!"

"You should listen to him...," Cartwright interjects, "...he has good instincts and a lot of years on the force. If he says it's her, then it's her!"

"Those notes were malicious and intended to hurt, I can't believe Laura is that good of an actress," Palmer proclaims adamantly.

"Yet you already suspect that she loaned her key to your brother knowing what he intended to use it for," Carter states the obvious. "It isn't a great leap of faith to think she did other favours for your brother!"

"No! My brother wasn't even in the country when all that started," Palmer protests, his mind not able to accept even the possibility that Connor could have been behind his losing Zoe. "He was in Italy, working for me on a project with my foreman, Craig Stanley!"

"And was Laura already involved with your brother," Carter asks, already knowing intuitively that he is correct.

Palmer pushes both hands back through his hair and begins to pace back and forth.

It can't be true! Connor barely knew Zoe then...he fancied her, that was obvious...but enough to do this?!

No! Damn it no!

"You're wrong! They had only just started seeing each other. He wouldn't have had time to form that kind of hold on Laura!"

But Carter just shrugs his shoulders and turns his attention back to the whiteboard.

"You're wrong," Palmer declares again, only this time he doesn't sound so sure.

"And what about these," Carter asks, pointing to the amounts of money that Palmer had identified on Connor's bank statements.

"They were payments that Connor received around the time that each of my tenders failed," Palmer explains. "We think we know who they're from, but we have no way of proving it."

"Oh?" Cartwright mutters curiously.

"Yes. We think Snelson was paying him to copy my tenders, then modified them enough to pass them off as his own."

"And what makes you think that," Carter asks, narrowing his eyes at Palmer.

"So far, he's won most of the contracts that I lucked out on. Though not so much, now that we know Connor was selling me out!"

"So, this man Snelson, he's in the building trade I take it?"

Palmer looks at Carter like he is stating the obvious. "Of course. Why else would he want my tenders?"

"You'd be surprised what people sell to other people," is all Carter replies.

"So you're thinking that there may have been a go-between that paid my brother then sold the tenders on to Snelson?" Palmer shakes his head in disbelief. "That doesn't sound likely to me."

"I didn't say it's what happened, I'm merely making the point that at this stage we can't assume anything!"

"We?!" Palmer looks from Carter to Cartwright and back again. "There is no 'we'," he tells them firmly.

Pursing his lips, Carter continues to study the board. "Then I take it you don't want our help in confirming that Snelson is your man?"

Caught between wanting to know for sure and not wanting to get involved with the police, Palmer begins pacing again.

This doesn't feel right. I know Connor's dead and can't be harmed by anything they find, but it still feels like a betrayal.

"He's gone," Carter states having read Palmer accurately. "There's not a thing we can do to touch him now. But he can help us put away a crook."

Then Carter moves to stand in front of Palmer, deciding to take the man into his confidence.

"Did you know that Snelson's building company is majority owned by Jennings?" Carter asks him, his voice deadly soft.

"What!" Paling instantly, Palmer comes to an abrupt halt and has to catch his breath. "I told him never to get involved with Jennings again. And after what he went through, I didn't believe he would!"

"He may not have known," Carter informs him. "We only found out because we ran an in-depth review of all

Jennings' finances – and we're still not done."

"You're going after Jennings?"

"Yes. But that's information that needs to stay in this room. Do I have your word on that," Carter demands quietly.

Palmer nods, considering the implications. "I think he was behind an accident on one of my construction sites," he tells them. "One of my men admitted to having been contacted by someone from his organisation."

"And how do you know he came from Jennings?" Carter asks with interest.

"Because it's something that Jennings would do. It's his kind of tactic and his method or choice," Palmer states confidently. "I've dealt with the man, I have a good idea how he works."

"So you think he's coming after you?"

"I think you annoyed the hell out of him and he blames me for it," Palmer frowns at the two men.

"Maybe so...," Carter concedes with a nod, "...which is another good reason to help us put him away."

Taking a seat in the lounge area, Palmer waves a hand to indicate that the two men should do the same.

"You should know that my friend, who has been helping me to figure this thing out, actually believes that Hickey beat my brother almost to death without Jennings' approval," Palmer tells them. "Hence why Jennings murdered then dumped Hickey's body on my doorstep. Craig thinks it was some sort of a macabre peace offering."

"So why did you tell us about him," Carter asks curiously.

"Because ultimately, Jennings is the one responsible for Connor's death. Another killing in no way makes up for that," Palmer states adamantly, his teeth gritted with the hate he feels towards Jennings.

"Couldn't agree more," Carter nods, then looks at Palmer with narrowed, speculative eyes. "So what's your plan...and please, don't insult my intelligence by telling me you haven't considered how to get back at Jennings, because I won't believe you."

Palmer returns Carter's look, weighing up just how much he can trust these men.

"Oh I've thought about it," Palmer admits. "I've even dreamed I beat him to a barely breathing pulp like his lackey did to Connor. But no...," Palmer holds up a staying hand when Cartwright sits up straighter in his seat, "...I don't have a plan to murder the cretin, even if he does deserve it!"

With a low chuckle, Carter leans back in his seat and looks at Palmer with a reluctant admiration.

CHAPTER NINE

"So will you help us," Cartwright asks.

"I believe we can take this man down for a very long time if we go about it in the right way," Carter adds his weight to Cartwright's request.

Rubbing his dry lips with the back of his hand, Palmer weighs up his options.

If I try to set Jennings up on my own using Sean to bring him out, I could fail. I might not get the proof I'd need to turn him over to the police and get him locked up.

And isn't that the point...I'd be turning him over to the police anyway...why not use them to help trap him?

But what about Sean...I don't want him getting into trouble because he was dumb enough to take money from Jennings. How do I know I wouldn't have done the same in his situation? It must be heart-breaking to see your once vibrant daughter stuck in a wheelchair and know that she has a chance to walk if you could just get the money together.

Shit!

"Coffee gentlemen...?" Palmer surprises them by offering as he gets to his feet and crosses to switch the kettle on.

"Do we have something more to discuss?" Carter asks with a lifted brow.

"We do," Palmer turns and smiles. "We most definitely do!"

When Zoe gets up she realises that she has slept the night through and her bladder is in urgent need of emptying.

Waddling quickly to the bathroom she only just makes it in time.

Damn my waterworks! Since I got heavier I can't seem to go long before I'm desperate for a pee again. You have something to answer for, Brook Johnson!

A few minutes later she comes out of the bathroom and bumps right into Craig coming out of her mother's bedroom.

"Oh! Sorry...I...sorry," she blathers nervously, not quite knowing what to say.

But Craig just gives her a wide smile and takes hold of

her shoulders to steady her.

"No problem. You're more likely to hurt yourself than me," he grins. "I'm made of tougher stuff."

"Yes, I can see that," she smiles and lifts a brow at his naked muscular chest.

With a chuckle, he continues into the bathroom and Zoe knocks on her mother's bedroom door before entering.

Her mother is sitting up in bed with a smile as wide as an ocean, and looking very satisfied with herself...or something.

"That man is a mountain of muscles," Zoe whispers as she sits on her mother's bed. "I just bumped right into him and he didn't even blink."

Carly leans back and continues to grin like a Cheshire cat. "He certainly is all man," she proclaims tellingly.

"Mother!" Zoe exclaims, shocked and a little embarrassed by her mother's admission.

"Well, you always wanted me to find a man to be happy with," Carly raises a questioning brow. "Aren't you happy for us, darling?"

"Very," Zoe concedes. "It's just weird thinking of you...and...him...you know..."

"Then don't think about it," Carly smiles. "Just wish us well and make him feel at home."

Zoe frowns, looking at her mother with quizzical eyes. "Is he...at home," she clarifies when Carly, too, begins to frown.

"We've talked about him moving in," she admits shyly. "But nothing has been decided yet. I think he's waiting to see what you think of the idea."

"Me?" Zoe asks, startled to think that she is standing in the way of her mother's happiness. "Why on earth would he do that?!"

"Because he's a very considerate man, and he knows how much I've missed you and wanted you home," Carly explains. "I think Craig doesn't want you to feel that he's stepping into your place in our home and my heart. But you know that no one could ever do that...don't you?"

Lunging forward, as much as her swollen body will allow, Zoe gives her mother a hug.

"I'm so happy for you," Zoe tells her with tears in her voice. "If Craig can give you the love and happiness that you deserve, then he has my blessing to move in with you. Though I think he should make an honest woman of you," she adds with a grin as she pulls back to look at her mother.

"Been sayin' the same thing myself," Craig surprises them, having moved very quietly for such a large man.

Grinning wildly, Zoe looks from one to the other and

gets up off the bed. "And...?"

Carly blushes deeply to the roots of her hair. "And I'm too old to be a bride," she declares putting a hand to her hot cheeks.

"Nonsense! You'd make me the proudest man alive," Craig smiles coaxingly.

"And I could help you organise the wedding," Zoe offers, bursting with excitement.

As Carly hesitates, Craig moves across the room and takes out a small box from the bedside table. Then he drops to one knee and holds it out towards Carly.

"Carly Benson, I have asked you before and now I am asking again in the presence of your daughter, will you do me the very great honour of becoming my wife?"

With tears brimming in her eyes and her bottom lip trembling badly, Zoe watches her mother reach out a hand to touch Craig's face.

"I would be proud to be your wife. So, yes, and thank you for loving me with such a kind heart," she tells him, before sealing their pact with a kiss.

Moving discretely out of the room, Zoe closes the bedroom door and goes back to her room to dress.

My mum is getting married! Oh my Lord! I wonder if Craig has told Palmer that he wants to marry mum?

Oh no, will he have Palmer as his best man? I bet he

will, they've been friends for years and I'm sure Palmer said that Craig doesn't have much in the way of family.

Dressed and ready for the day ahead, Zoe makes her way downstairs and into the kitchen to make a cup of tea.

I don't know what's wrong with that man, first Palmer chases me all the way to Looe and then he can't get away from me fast enough! And they say women are fickle!

Pouring the boiling water into the teapot, Zoe makes enough for her mother and Craig too, just in case they actually come down any time soon.

With a grin, she takes a mug of tea out to the patio and enjoys the early morning sun.

"Hey, good morning to you too," she tells her baby having felt her kick. "You'll be sitting out here with mummy very soon now. I can't wait to see your beautiful face."

With a hand smoothing gently over her stomach, Zoe thinks of her baby's father.

Is that it, Palmer...you just wanted me back here so that you could see our daughter when she arrives? Was all that profession of love just another lie?

"You look very content," her mother surprises her, stepping out onto the patio with a cup of tea.

"Where's Craig?" Zoe asks, expecting the big man to be with her mother.

"I think he's giving us a little time to talk," Carly tells her mysteriously.

"Talk? Is something wrong?"

"No, no, nothing's wrong," Carly smiles, quick to reassure her daughter. "But I asked Craig to move in with us, and he will...but only if it won't make you uncomfortable."

"Mum, no, it won't make me uncomfortable to see you two happy. I like Craig, and I think he's good for you."

With a bright smile, Carly gets up and goes back inside the house then returns with Craig at her side.

"You two look great together," Zoe laughs, her slight mother looking positively delicate next to the man mountain she is to marry.

Craig bends to place a kiss on Zoe's cheek. "Thanks for givin' us your blessing — I know it means a lot to your mum, as it does to me too."

"I couldn't be happier for both of you," Zoe grins as the happy couple take a seat at the patio table. "When do you think you'll get married?"

Looking doe eyed at each other, her mother blushes and says, "Well, I don't want a big wedding — just something small and intimate with close family. So it shouldn't take too much organising."

Craig nods his large head in agreement.

"I'm ready whenever you are, you know that," he grins happily.

Raising a finger in the air, Zoe gets their attention. "Can I be really selfish and ask you to wait until Brook arrives. I would just like to not look like a beached whale on the wedding photos, if you can wait that long."

With a girlish giggle that makes Zoe grin, Carly agrees. "It will take at least that long to get everything arranged." Then looking deep into her future husband's eyes, she says, "I've always thought Christmas weddings must be magical..."

"Then Christmas it is," Craig agrees readily.

"I've thought about offering to work for Palmer again," Zoe tells them out of the blue. "It would be good for me to get out of the house. You know I'm not good at just sitting around," she tells her mother.

"But, Zoe..."

"That sounds like a great idea," Craig interjects when her mother would have objected. "As long as you take your time and rest up when you get home."

Giving Craig a grateful smile, Zoe turns hopeful eyes to her mother. She knows she doesn't need her approval, but it would be nice to have it all the same.

"I suppose... I worked right up to the end of my pregnancy with you," Carly admits. "So it would be hypocritical of me to tell you not to. But take care of yourself and the baby, Zoe. That's all I ask."

Jumping to her feet, Zoe grins down at both of them. "I'll go and give Palmer a ring right now! Won't he be surprised!"

But Craig holds up a staying hand and says, "No need. I'm working the office just now, and I say you can start whenever you're ready."

For some unknown reason, Zoe is crestfallen. *Well, hell!*

"That's great...thank you," she smiles, retaking her seat and finishing her tea.

But Craig can see her disappointment and feels a ray of hope for his friend's relationship.

I don't know why I'm so put out; surely this is better than asking Palmer for a job? He'd have probably said no anyway!

But, damn it, I wanted to speak to him. Now I don't have any reason to call!

"Are you ok?" Carly asks with a worried frown. "You look lost in thought."

"Just thinking about work...the changes...you know."

Like Palmer not being in the office while I'm working! I didn't realise Craig was in there all the time.

Why is that? There's something going on!

"You'll be fine," Craig smiles reassuringly. "You hired Mandy before you left, so at least you know each other."

"That's true...," she frowns, deep in thought, "...but won't she mind if I step back into my old role?"

"Not at all. I know she has been feelin' the stress a bit lately," Craig tells her. "I think she will be more than happy to hand the reigns back over to you!"

"Ok. Well, if you're sure I'd like to start back on Monday."

Nodding his large head, Craig smiles with a secret glee.

But come Monday, Zoe is beginning to have second thoughts.

This is crazy! He won't even be there, why are you so damned nervous!

Standing in front of the mirror, she holds up yet another dress and cringes.

They're all just tents in different fabrics! How the hell am I supposed to look like an efficient PA in any of these!

But there's no choice, she has to wear one of them.

With her hair tied back in a very long ponytail and just a little makeup, Zoe walks into her old office and is glad that Mandy has yet to arrive.

Phew, that's a relief! Ok, so let's see if the passwords are the same... Yes! I can get started catching up with what's been going on and finding my feet again.

For the next hour, Zoe goes through the computer and the files that are on her desk.

That's odd...I don't remember Palmer losing out on so many tenders before. I wonder what went wrong.

Digging even deeper now that she is on the scent of something, Zoe is shocked to see just how many tenders Palmer had failed to secure jobs on.

Was this my fault? Was he so wrapped up in trying to get me back that he messed up?

No, that doesn't sound like Palmer at all. But then perhaps he really hasn't been himself what with everything that's happened?

Christ, I am one selfish woman! I've put Palmer through agonies and his company has suffered for it. Now what do I do – I can't exactly pretend that I don't know about it?

CHAPTER TEN

Studying his whiteboard with a mug of coffee in hand, Palmer tries to see the information from an outsider's point of view.

If they're right and Laura was at the back of those notes all along... Damn it! I wish they hadn't put that thought in my head, now I can't think round it!

They must have got that wrong – Laura and Zoe were tight, best buddies!

But if I were Carter...yes, I can see where he's coming from alright. And it does make a macabre sort of sense.

Love, some people will do anything for it. Even commit murder in some extreme cases.

And this is not extreme at all when I really think about it. She was crazy about Connor right from the off – Zoe said so, and she'd be a pretty good judge, I think.

Taking a step back, Palmer once again goes through dates, the timing of the notes and then remembers something pretty damning.

"You god-damned-bitch! It was you," he exclaims as he recalls what Zoe had told him. "You took delivery of those roses and you put the note and photos with them for Zoe to find!"

Spinning away from the board, Palmer can't believe how stupid he's been. It was right there, smack in front of his eyes the whole time. But he'd been too blind to see it.

Well, not anymore! I see who you are now, and I'm coming for you, Laura!

When Craig arrives in the office, he finds Zoe with her head bent over some files, deep in concentration.

"Mornin'," he smiles, striding over to his office door. But when she doesn't reply he looks back with concern. "You alright?" he asks, moving to look over her shoulder at what seems to have captivated her attention.

"I did this," she tells him, and realises that he knows full well what she's talking about when she looks up at Craig. "Why didn't he tell me that things were this bad?"

Deciding not to set her straight about what has been going on, and Connor's role in it, Craig walks back to his office door.

"You know Palmer better than that. He'd never use

emotional blackmail to get you back," he states knowingly.

Then he goes into his office and leaves Zoe to think about that.

No, Craig's right, Palmer would never do that. But did he need to exclude me so entirely!

But then she realises how stupid her thoughts are and how wrong she's been.

He didn't exclude me...I did that all by myself. I was so wrapped up in my own little world that I didn't give a thought to the mess I was leaving behind.

But now what? I can't exactly say 'Hi Palmer, I know you nearly lost you company because I was so selfish'! But it's true.

And what if he has been telling the truth all along? What if those photos turn out to be fake? Oh my God, what if all this was my own stupid fault for believing some anonymous bitch that just wanted my man! Wouldn't that be the kicker of all time!

Then Zoe gets the shock of her life, and gives Palmer one too when he strides to his office door and marches through it after giving her a look that could kill.

"What the hell is Zoe doing here?" he demands of Craig the minute the door is shut.

"She wanted a job, I told her she could start back just

as soon as she was ready. She's ready," Craig smiles annoyingly.

"Well I didn't tell her she could have her old job back!" Palmer paces the floor in front of his desk where Craig is leaning back in his seat smiling up at him. "What the fuck are you smiling at?" he demands harshly.

"I'm smilin' at you," Craig chuckles deeply. "You are like a bear with a sore head. What's got you so riled up? And don't tell me it's all because of Zoe, I know you better than that," the big man frowns, his smile fading.

Coming to a stop and looking down at the best friend he's ever had, Palmer hauls in a large breath and tries to let it out slowly.

Then he utters one word. "Laura!"

Nodding slowly, not taking his eyes off his friend, Craig sits forward in his seat.

"I wondered how long it would take you to work it out," he tells Palmer quietly.

"You... What the hell, Craig! You knew it was Laura all along?" Palmer asks, stunned by the thought.

"I had my suspicions, but I had to see if you came to the same conclusion," he explains, his deep, brown voice trailing off into a sigh.

"Why? You were quick enough to point out that Laura was the most likely candidate to have loaned her keys to

Connor – so why not tell me about the notes," he pushes, confused that his friend had held back such important information.

"It took you a while to accept the key theory, and I can understand why," Craig states in a conciliatory tone. "She's worked for you for a few years now, you've never had any problem with her work and she was Zoe's friend."

"But...," Palmer pushes again when Craig hesitates.

"But it's the only thing that really makes sense, and that means that Connor was behind it the whole time," Craig sighs, pointing out the obvious.

Almost falling into the seat opposite Craig, Palmer rubs his hands over his tired face.

"He must have hated me pretty bad to have done all of this," Palmer murmurs, raising his head to look across the desk at Craig. "Was I such a bad brother?" he asks, shaking his head in disbelief.

"I don't think Connor hated you, not really," the big man tells him. "I think what you told me about how your parents always pushed him to be like you just ate away at him a piece at a time. He couldn't live up to you so he went the opposite way – he blew his inheritance and refused to conform. This wasn't all about you," he assures Palmer.

With a sceptical chuckle, Palmer shakes his head, "You

have no idea how much I would love to believe that. I would have done just about anything to turn Connor around." With his head bowed, Palmer murmurs, "I still can't believe he's gone."

"Hmm, well right now we have a problem to deal with," Craig states, trying to distract Palmer from his morose thoughts.

When Palmer looks up at him, Craig can see that he has succeeded.

"Yes, damn it, we do! I'll be back in just a moment," Palmer grinds out, his blue eyes like ice when he marches out of the office and past a stunned Zoe.

However, she is even more stunned to see Palmer frogmarching her friend into his office and rises to her feet to protest.

But Palmer gets in first. "Not now, Zoe! You have no idea what's been going on!"

And with that he closes the door with an uncharacteristic bang.

What the hell! He can't treat Laura like that – she looked terrified!

But deep inside, Zoe knows that Palmer must have good reason for his actions.

This isn't like Palmer at all, he's a good boss. He's usually kind and concerned for his employees...I just don't get it. What could Laura have done to get him so mad?

Laura does, indeed, look terrified when she is told to sit in the seat opposite Craig.

The two men are looking at her like something nasty they just stepped in.

"I don't under...understand," she stammers nervously. "I haven't done anything wrong. Ask Mr Spears, he'll tell you I do good work," she pleads when both her bosses just continue to stare at her.

"No doubt," Palmer finally speaks, having dragged his temper under control. "But then he doesn't know about the keys you lent to Connor," Palmer states, and watches Laura begin to relax when she thinks this is what she is here for.

After all, they didn't sack her the last time they spoke to her about that incident, so why would they do so now.

"I've apologised for that, and I'm really sorry for what happened...," she pleads, "...but I thought you were giving me another chance."

"Yes...we did do that, didn't we?" Palmer murmurs, looking at her like an insect under a microscope. "You must have had a good laugh at that," he smiles grimly. "I'll bet you thought you'd gotten away with it all scot free!"

"B.but, I d.don't understand..."

Shifting in her seat, Laura begins to feel like a hammer

is about to fall on her head and she can't work out why.

"Then understand this!" Craig snaps, causing her head to whip round and look at him. "We know all about your involvement with the notes that Zoe received. And we know that Connor put you up to it!"

Watching as all the colour leaves Laura's face, Craig doesn't have it in him to feel pity for her. Laura has caused so much pain and heartache, he thinks it's high time she realised what it's like.

Silence. For a whole 30 seconds the room went quiet and Laura trembles with fear.

"How could you do it," Palmer asks softly. "You were her friend, how could you do that to Zoe?" he demands, his voice hard as ice.

But instead of buckling beneath the accusation, Laura amazes them both by lifting her chin in defiance.

"I did it because I'm Zoe's friend," she declares hotly, having found her own anger. "Connor told me what you were up to – he told me all about the affairs you were having behind Zoe's back!"

Closing his eyes on the pain of that revelation, Palmer has to accept that this was mostly Connor's doing.

"I know what my brother did...," Palmer tells her, "...and I know what you did. He lied and you believed him, but it was Zoe that got hurt in the process!"

Shaking her head, not wanting to believe him, Laura shouts, "You're a liar! Connor showed me those photos, you were right there kissing that woman! Don't come the innocent with me...you're the one to blame for all this!"

But Palmer is done; he's had enough of trying to defend himself and won't bring himself to do so to this creature!

"You'd better clear your desk and leave before I put my hands round your neck and throttle you," he threatens angrily. "Get out!" he shouts when she doesn't immediately move, and watches in disgust as she runs from the room.

"Laura?" Zoe gasps as she watches her friend dash by in tears. Then she marches over to the still open office door and demands, "What the hell is going on? Why is Laura in tears?"

"Damn it, Zoe, not now!" Palmer snaps, then lifts his hands and lets them fall in despair.

"Come on in...," Craig waves a hand to beckon Zoe, "...and shut the door please."

Doing so, Zoe crosses the room and takes the now vacant seat. Then, looking at Craig, she asks, "Ok, now will you explain?"

Glancing up at Palmer, Craig can see that he is in no fit state to do that so he does his best to tell it like it is.

"We found out who was behind the notes you were receiving," Craig tells her softly. But when she merely tilts her head to one side and frowns he expounds. "Apparently, Connor convinced Laura that Palmer was having an affair and she went along with the scheme."

"What?! You can't be serious!" she gapes, looking from Craig to a very distraught Palmer. "Palmer, this is crazy talk, you can't go around accusing people like that! It's...it's criminal!"

Rounding on her, Palmer has a tough time reigning in his temper. After all, it isn't Zoe he's really angry with. But to hear her defend her so-called-friend, makes him seethe!

But Craig feels his pain and knows it will only get worse if he takes it out on Zoe.

Holding up a large hand to Palmer, Craig says, "Hold it, boss! Just calm down before you say somthin' you're sure to regret. And she ain't worth it," he adds to Zoe's surprise.

"Not you, too!"

"Listen, Princess," Craig growls gently, using his new nickname for his soon to be step-daughter, "we just heard it from Laura's own lips. Connor seems to have convinced her that the photos were genuine and, in her own twisted way, she thought telling you was the right thing to do.

Sorry," he adds when he sees her hurt expression.

"Laura... It was Laura...?" she asks inanely.

Hearing the hurt in her voice immediately calms Palmer down. "I'm sorry, Zoe. I didn't see it until it was staring me in the face. If only I'd seen it sooner, things may not have gone this far."

And maybe we'd already be married, like we should be! That woman has a lot to answer for. Whether she believed Connor or not, it doesn't excuse her actions. Leaving anonymous notes for Zoe to find was just cruel.

"Where is she, I need to go talk with her!" And standing quickly, Zoe makes to leave the room. But when she tries to put one foot in front of the other Zoe suddenly feels faint.

"Christ!" Palmer gasps, reaching out to steady her and guide her back down in her seat. Crouching down in front of her, Palmer searches her face for signs of anything seriously wrong.

"Zoe? Just take some deep breaths and lean back in the chair. That's it...good girl...slow and deep...slow and deep."

Looking over at Craig, Palmer's eyes are now lit with anger. "Make sure she's gone. I don't want her hanging around to upset Zoe!"

With a nod of agreement, Craig moves round the desk

and lays a large, gentle hand on Zoe's shoulder before he goes.

"Are you sure...? Are you really sure?" Zoe's eyes plead for Palmer to tell her it isn't true, but she can see from his pained expression that it is. "Ok. Ok. At least now we know there isn't some maniac stalker out there waiting for me in the shadows!"

"Jesus, Zoe, is that what you thought?!"

"Well it could have been! Spurned women have been known to murder their rivals," she states, relieved that it's all over.

"How are you feeling? Should I get you some water...or anything else?" he asks.

But Zoe just shakes her head. "I'm fine. Or I will be, just as soon as the reality of all this sinks in." Reaching out to Palmer, Zoe touches his cheek. "It must have gotten ugly in here, I'm sorry you had to go through that."

Smiling, happy to feel her tender touch again, Palmer turns his lips into her palm.

"You're worth going through a hundred times worse for. I love you, Zoe. I need you to believe that," he tells her earnestly.

But a shadow crosses her face and he knows that she still has doubts.

Getting to his feet, Palmer shoves frustrated hands

back through his hair and begins pacing the floor.

"It's those damned photos," he exclaims angrily. "I've sent them to a lab for analysis, so you won't have long to wait before the truth finally bites you in the backside!"

And before she can utter another word, Palmer strides out of the office leaving her world in turmoil.

I want to believe you, Palmer. I want that so much...but the photos. Even you said it was you with that woman in the picture....

<u>CHAPTER ELEVEN</u>

When the police call Palmer asking for a meeting at his place, along with Craig and Sean, he begins to worry that his men are getting dragged in too deep.

"Will you stop acting like a mother hen," Craig frowns over at Palmer. "We can take care of ourselves...," he proclaims, jabbing a large finger into his own chest then pointing it at Sean, "...and this is the right thing to do. You know that!"

"I don't want either of you taking risks," Palmer states obstinately. "You don't need to tell me that you're grown men, but I'm your boss and I don't want either of you getting hurt on account of a creep like Jennings!"

"Boss, I'm not just here because I owe you," Sean tries to explain. "Though I know I owe you big time. But Craig's right...this is the right thing to do. Connor is probably not the first or last person to lose their life because of Jennings. If we can help to get him locked away, I think we have a duty to try."

Just then, a loud knock come at the front door and Palmer crosses the loft to open it.

"Good to see you, gentlemen," Carter greets them all with a grim smile.

"What's up, you look tense?" Palmer asks as the two detectives cross the room to take a seat with Craig and Sean.

"We found a body in the early hours of this morning," Cartwright informs them gravely. "Looks like Jennings' new henchman isn't as good at covering his tracks the way Hickey used to. The lad was in his early twenties — apparently his crime was bad mouthing Jennings in a public place!"

"Christ!" Craig growls and looks up at Palmer with determination in his eyes. "You see what we're sayin'; that man needs bringing down and we're going to see that it gets done!"

Nodding silently, Palmer joins the group by taking a seat in the lounge area.

"Ok, let's work this out. I gather you have come up with a plan," Palmer looks from Carter to Cartwright with an expectant lift of his brow.

Nodding, Carter looks over at Sean then asks, "Did you say what we told you? Have you got a face-to-face meet with Jennings?"

"Yes. I said it just like you told me – I wasn't going to trust a couple of goons to give me orders or ask me to do dangerous stuff. If Jennings wants me to work for him, he can tell me himself," Sean repeats, then gives a relieved smile. "I never knew I could act – maybe I have options for a stage career I never knew about."

They all chuckle at the joke, but every man there knows that what they're planning to do is not a laughing matter.

"Ok," Carter nods with approval. "We'll hook you up with the latest wire and then we can get him on tape." But Carter hesitates before continuing with the plan. "Are you sure you're up for this – it's not too late to call it off."

Looking surprised by the offer, Sean shakes his head vigorously. "No, I want to do this. We can't let that maniac ruin our city!"

"You have a family..." Carter reminds him.

"Yes, I do. And I'd be doing this for them. I don't want my daughter growing up with gangsters on her doorstep. What kind of a dad would that make me," he asks Carter.

"A brave one, I'd say," Carter acknowledges with a slow nod of his head.

"I couldn't agree more," Palmer tells him, and sees a weight lift off of Sean as his spine straightens. "You're a good man, Sean. Don't think you have anything to prove. If you want to step aside from this, no one will think any the less of you."

"Thanks, boss. That means a lot," Sean tells him sincerely. "But I'm fine with this. I meant what I said; I want this creep off the streets as much as anyone here."

"Sounds like we have a lot to talk about," Palmer smiles at the group of men. "I'm going to take a second to stick the kettle on then we can get down to it."

"I should tell you all that the reason we wanted to meet here is because we've had a tail on us from the day we brought Jennings in for questioning," Carter announces to them all. "He's obviously worried what we'll find out."

"But you'd have to be blind not to spot them," Cartwright adds, a note of disgust in his gruff voice.

"True. They're obviously amateurs, and that's to our advantage," Carter smiles.

"So, what difference did meetin' here make," Craig sits forward, concern in his eyes.

"Don't worry. We drove out of the station in our usual vehicle then switched cars in a multi storey car park," Carter chuckles with a shake of his head. "They're probably still there waiting for us to come back out."

"Which we will...," Cartwright continues, "...once we've parked the switch car back where we got it from."

Coming back with a tray of mugs filled with black coffee, Palmer places it on the table in the middle of the seating area and lets everyone help themselves to milk and sugar.

"So you've known about your tail from the off?" Palmer asks as he retakes his seat.

"It wasn't difficult to spot them. They were virtually riding our bumper the whole time," Cartwright chuckles as he stirs sugar into his coffee.

"So, let's go over the plan," Carter says, getting everyone's attention.

For the next couple of hours the men go over every detail. Nothing is left to chance.

"The surveillance team have already picked up on the feed for Jennings' own hidden camera system. Whatever he sees we'll see," Carter assures Sean. "We'll be watching you the whole time and we'll be in there at the first sign of trouble."

Nodding, Sean doesn't seem fazed at all.

"So you're watching him already," Craig asks for clarification.

"Have been for a while," Cartwright tells them. "He's a

jerk, and the men he's got working for him are real losers. Serves him right for offing Hickey!"

When Zoe gets home from work she tells her mother all about what happened at the office.

"Laura! I can hardly believe it," her mother gasps.

"Well didn't Craig tell you," Zoe asks wide eyed. "Where is the big guy; have you got him gardening or what?"

With a light chuckle, Carly dismisses the idea as ludicrous. "Craig is not the gardening type. He likes to sit in a nice garden alright, but you won't catch him weeding it!"

"Hmm, I don't know about that but he left the office before me so where did he go?" Zoe persists, full of curiosity.

"He said the police wanted a meeting with him, Palmer and Sean at Palmer's flat," Carly frowns. "Though I have no idea why they wanted it there and Craig didn't seem to know either."

"I hate all this trouble and secrecy...," Zoe grimaces, her hand stoking over her full womb lovingly, "...I have a really bad feeling about it." *Something is wrong, baby, I can feel it in my bones!*

"If the meeting is to discuss Connor's death, I don't see why Craig or Sean needs to be involved," Carly states with a frown.

Then her frown deepens and Carly tilts her head to listen. "That's your mobile," she tells Zoe, who doesn't appear to have noticed it ringing.

Reaching into her bag, Zoe looks at the caller ID and smiles brightly.

"Dad! Hi, are you ok, is your latest movie going alright," she bubbles exuberantly.

Looking at her mother, Zoe's grin widens. "Mum's fine, and yes she is as beautiful as ever," Zoe confirms and watches her mother blush. Then her eyes go round and she lets out an excited scream as she jumps to her feet, "You are, when?"

Carly gets up to give her daughter some privacy, but Zoe frantically signals for her to stay.

"You have! For six whole months! That's great, dad," Zoe exclaims with another excited squeal that makes her mother laugh and shake her head at her. "Ok, dad, see you soon. Yes, I will, bye."

When Zoe continues to gape at her open mouthed and wide eyed Carly gives her a playful poke.

"Are you ever going to tell me what he said?" she asks her daughter.

"Well, first I have to give you his love and best wishes and tell you that he thinks of you often," Zoe giggles, watching her mother squirm in her seat. "And he's coming over for six whole months at the end of this week! Can you believe it?!"

"What! Are you sure you heard him right?" Carly asks in disbelief.

"Absolutely! He said he's rented a house and wants to be here for Brook's birth and first Christmas," Zoe sighs and takes her seat again. "It will be my first Christmas with my dad, too," she smiles a little sadly. "At least, the first I will remember."

"He was always a good dad, Zoe," Carly smiles encouragingly. "He spoiled you rotten all the time, you were a real daddy's girl."

"I was?" Zoe brightens. "Well, we'll have lots of time to get to know each other properly again, and Brook will get to know her grandad."

"You've really opened your heart to him," Carly states with some surprise. "I wasn't sure that you would."

"I suppose the old bond is still there," Zoe smiles happily. "As soon as I met him it felt like I was whole again – well...almost."

Frowning with concern, Carly asks, "Almost, Zoe? What's worrying you?"

Rubbing nervous hands over her face, Zoe tries to put her feelings into words.

"It's Palmer. No matter how I try I can't get him out of

my head or my heart," she moans softly.

"You still love him," Carly smiles knowingly. "I always knew that when you loved you would love completely – it's who you are, Zoe. Just as you are with your dad."

"That doesn't seem to bother you so much," Zoe frowns at her mother. "At first, it was like you didn't want him back in my life."

"Because I was afraid he would hurt you again. That's the only reason," Carly assures her. "But the way he's helped you and kept in touch...well, I'm really impressed. I'm glad you two are getting on so well."

"Thanks mum."

"Now, tell me what you're going to do about Palmer," Carly demands gently.

"The trouble is, I'm not sure there's anything I can do. He seems so distant now that we're back in Birmingham," Zoe tells her mother with a confused frown.

"He was totally different in Cornwall – all loving and trying to convince me that he was never unfaithful," she huffs, lifting her palms in the air and letting them fall back into her lap. "But he's changed. I'm not sure he even wants me anymore."

"Yet he took off to Cornwall the minute he heard you were ill," Carly reminds her. "That isn't the act of a man that no longer cares."

"Maybe he was worried about Brook?" Zoe speculates quietly. "He barely even looks at me these days."

"Hmm, I must admit I thought he would be round here every night," Carly muses. "But all this has been hard on Palmer, too. Have you ever considered that he could be completely innocent of all those horrid accusations?"

With raised brows, Zoe looks at her mother in amazement. "But what about the photos? Even he said it was him with that woman!"

"What?!" Carly gapes in stunned surprise. "He actually admitted that?"

"Well, no," Zoe tries to explain. "He said that it was him in the photo but that he had never even met the woman, let alone kissed her. And that he would never do that to me," she finishes on a heavy sigh.

"Did you believe him?" Carly asks, and Zoe looks at her in disbelief.

"But it was right there on the photos..."

"That isn't what I asked you," Carly persists. "I asked if you believed him when he told you that he'd never met that woman or ever been unfaithful to you."

"I don't know..."

"Yes, you do," Carly insists firmly. "In your heart you know the truth; have the courage to admit that even if it's only to yourself."

Getting up, Zoe begins to pace back and forth in front of her mother, then comes to a sudden stop.

"When he told me, when he looked me in the eyes and told me that it wasn't true, I didn't see a lie," she admits. "But I'm just not sure whether I believed him because that's what I wanted to believe. And in the end, I couldn't trust it so I let him go," she sighs, and sits back down.

For endless moments, mother and daughter simply look at each other and speak volumes without the need for words.

"I got this all wrong, didn't I?" Zoe heaves a heavy sigh. "If I truly love Palmer, then I should trust him. Photos be damned, I should have trusted him."

"Only you can decide that," Carly tells her. "But you said that Palmer had sent them to be analysed at a photography lab; hasn't he heard back from them yet?"

"No," Zoe shakes her head in despair.

"Good," Carly states, surprising Zoe no end. "Then I suggest you tell Palmer how you feel before that happens."

"But, why..."

"Because he needs to know you trust him because of who he is and not just because you have indisputable proof!"

"Oh. Oh!" she exclaims louder, realising the importance of what her mother just said. "Yes, your right. Oh, mum, what if I'm too late? What if he really doesn't want me anymore?"

With a soft chuckle, Carly shakes her head. "I don't think you need worry about that. Palmer visited us a few times while you were away and he never showed any signs that his love for you was waning."

"Ok. I'll tell him first chance I get," Zoe decides, and feels a weight lift from her heart.

<u>CHAPTER TWELVE</u>

The day starts just like any other. Sean kisses his wife and daughter goodbye and makes his way to the building site and work.

A couple of undercover policemen have arrived dressed in work gear and are mixing a batch of cement.

"Morning," Sean greets his men as he passes them, and does the same to the officers. Then he continues on his way into the site office.

"Jesus!" Sean exclaims when he walks in and finds Jennings' men already sitting in his office. "What the hell?"

"Mr Jennings would like to have that chat now," the gorilla in a suit tells him.

"Well I can't make it right now," Sean procrastinates, knowing that he needs to give the undercover officers a signal that the meet is on and is happening right now.

But the gorilla and his smaller mate move forward with a look of determination on their faces.

"Mr Jennings says now, so you come now," the gorilla tells Sean.

"I'm not saying I won't come...," Sean placates, "...but if I don't go out there and give my men their instructions for the job it will draw attention to my leaving. And I don't think your Mr Jennings would be very pleased about that!"

The gorilla appears to give it some thought, then nods and grunts to give Sean permission to go outside.

Keeping his walk natural and approaching his own men first, Sean gives them the plans for the day then turns to the undercover officers.

"You two, I expect you to listen carefully," he tells them cryptically. "This site is dangerous and I won't be around to hold your hand. You got me...?" he asks, praying that they do.

"Yes sir." Officer Cooper nods. "We'll be on our guard and listening closely. No problem."

Sean follows Jennings' men to their car and climbs in the back seat when the gorilla holds the door open for him.

Christ! I hope I can pull this off. Cooper and Rogers

looked like they understood; I just have to hope Jennings doesn't get suspicious.

Even before the car pulls away, Officers Cooper and Rogers spring into action and alert the observation van parked near to Jennings' bar to be on the lookout for Sean's arrival.

Both Craig and Palmer are seated in the observation van, having insisted on being present. And they exchange concerned looks when they hear the call come through.

"Looks like your friend came through," a young officer nearest to Palmer smiles.

"Sean's a good man, be sure your men come through for him if he needs it," Palmer frowns back at the officer, his eyes full of concern.

"You don't need to worry about that..." the young officer continues to smile, "...not with Detective Carter on the job. He's tops!"

Palmer looks at Craig, "Sounds like we got the best, anyway."

"Sounds like," Craig's deep voice rumbles.

A message comes in over the radio.

"They should be with you in 10," the disembodied voice informs them. "Traffic out here is end to end, but it's moving."

"Ok, we'll be watching," another officer replies. "Just

to be clear...," the same officer turns to look at Craig and Palmer, "...if we need to exit the van to provide back-up, you stay put! Is that understood?"

Again, Craig and Palmer look at each other and speak volumes without words.

"Got it," Palmer states, and Craig nods in agreement.

The officer looks at them suspiciously, sure he had detected some hidden agenda in the look the two men had exchanged. But there was nothing he could do except watch them carefully.

After a few minutes they observe the car with Sean in the back pull up outside Jennings' bar. The two goons get out and open the back door then escort Sean inside.

"Ok. We've got eyes and ears," the radio officer announces. "And we're recording for the record."

They listen to the cackle and ribbing that goes on as the three men march through a small crowd of patrons to the back office.

Everyone in the van is watching the monitor with bated breath as Sean steps into the lion's den.

"And there he is...," Palmer stares daggers into the screen, "...just as cocky and laid back as usual."

Sean is working hard to calm his racing heart beat as he steps further into the room.

"So, you wouldn't take my men's word for a job I want

you to do," Jennings states, leaning back in his leather chair and staring up at Sean. "Why is that, I wonder?"

"From the little they told me, it sounded big. I'm not taking those kind of orders from anyone but you," Sean states convincingly, looking Jennings straight in the eyes.

Not moving a muscle, Jennings continues to watch Sean, looking for any sign of deceit.

"If you're not being straight with me, I can promise you you'll pay dearly for it," Jennings tells him, his voice cold and quiet.

"I did the last job alright, didn't I," Sean frowns, seemingly offended by Jennings' accusation.

Again, Jennings does nothing but watch Sean carefully. Then he sits forward in his seat and points to the chair on the opposite side of his desk.

"Take a seat. And stop getting all bent out of shape – I just want to be sure you understand the consequences of crossing me," Jennings smiles caustically.

"I know the score, and so do you," Sean states bravely. "I need the money for my girl, so let's stop beating around the bush here!"

Nodding, Jennings looks at Sean with reluctant admiration.

I could really use a man like this. He has needs that I can use to bend him to my will. And he's got smarts too. I doubt he'd take on Hickey's former role, but you never know what a desperate man will do for the right damount of money!

"You've got some balls, I'll give you that," Jennings chuckles softly. "Now we'll find out just how big they are."

For an endless moment the two men weigh each other up.

"I'd do almost anything to see my daughter walk again," Sean tells Jennings sincerely. "As long as that doesn't include murder, I'm in!"

Just as I thought, but we'll see in time.

"Nothing as drastic as that," Jennings informs Sean as he leans back in his seat again. "Just a few accidents at work, nothing fatal."

Sean frowns deeply, hoping the cops are getting all of this on tape so that he doesn't have to follow through.

"You want me to hurt my own men?" he asks bluntly.

"Just a few accidents," Jennings repeats. "Enough to bring Health and Safety down on your boss' head for a while! That should keep him busy and out of my damned hair!"

"I don't get it...," Sean frowns in confusion, "...you're not even in the building trade, what difference would that make to you?"

"What I am in, or not in, is none of your damned

business!" Jennings growls quietly, keeping a tight leash on his temper. "You just do as I say and everything will be alright!"

"I don't care what you're into," Sean continues, not backing down in the slightest. "I'm only interested in the money and you still haven't told me what I'm going to be paid."

Back in the van the radio officer lets out a long breath. "Just stay calm and keep it real," he advises Sean as if he can hear him.

"I think he's playin' it just right," Craig smiles admiringly. "Jennings doesn't want a yes man, he wants someone he can mould into his right hand man. And he's interviewing Sean for the job, if you ask me."

All eyes turn to Craig, including Palmer's.

"You think?"

"Those bozos he's got workin' for him ain't worth shit! I know his kind, he wants Sean on his team – this isn't about him doing a job, it's a test," Craig states confidently.

"You might be right," the radio officer nods in agreement. "Not that Hickey was any kind of brain-of-Britain, but at least he had some smarts. Those two are about as useful as Tweedledee and Tweedledum!"

A chuckle of appreciation breaks out between the men in the van.

Then they fall silent as Jennings begins to talk again.

"I paid you £5K for leaving a door unlocked," Jennings reminds him. "I'm willing to double that for some hands on this time."

"10K...," Sean frowns in disgust, "...you expect me to hurt my men and risk prosecution for just 10K!"

Swinging from side to side in his chair, Jennings continues to weigh up the man in front of him.

"Ok. I'll double that if you agree to work for me from now on and you'll get 5K a month as a retainer," Jennings smiles, obviously thinking he's just made Sean an offer he won't be able to turn down.

Sean looks at Jennings suspiciously. "Do I have to give my job up completely?"

"Not at all," Jennings tells him placatingly. "You're my inside man. I want to know anything Johnson says about the investigation into his brother's death. Or Hickey's, come to that!"

"And that's it. You just want information, no killing people, or shit like that?"

Feeling pleased with himself for getting Sean on board, Jennings actually laughs.

"I've got other people for that kind of stuff," he dismisses easily. "Just take care of the accidents on site and we'll take it from there."

Much later, when Sean, Craig, and the two detectives meet up with Palmer at his flat, there is an air of relief that the meeting with Jennings had passed without incident.

Giving Sean a slap on the back Craig says, "I agree with Jennings, you have really got some whopping balls!" Then everyone laughs as Sean has to catch the breath that's just been knocked out of him.

"Damn straight," Palmer agrees, leading the way across the room to the lounge area.

"You don't think I over did it?" Sean asks.

"Not at all," Carter and Cartwright say in unison to the amusement of the group.

"Well, I for one feel glad that it's all over," Palmer sighs heavily. "Anyone fancy a drink?"

Much to Palmer's surprise, everyone opts for coffee. "Right then, I'll put the kettle on."

A few minutes later they are all chatting about the outcome of Sean's meeting with Jennings.

"But why do you want him to continue...," Palmer asks, concerned for his man, "...surely you got enough to haul his arse into prison. He virtually admitted that he pays for murder to be done at his behest – what more do you need?"

"We want to get him for more than just solicitation of

a criminal act," Carter states firmly. "So far, all we've got is Jennings admitting to paying Sean to leave a door unlocked and offering to pay him to cause a few petty accidents. A good lawyer will get him off almost scot free!"

"Christ!" Palmer bites out angrily.

"It's alright, boss...," Sean reassures him, "...I want to bring that gutter rat down. Whatever I can do, I'm glad to do it."

"We'll stage the accidents, of course," Carter continues. "And we'll have a couple of officers in suits give you some grief as Health & Safety Inspectors," he smiles over at Palmer. "But we'll try not to hold you up too much – just enough to be convincing."

Nodding his ascent, Palmer considers the plan. "So you want Sean to pass on information to Jennings, and you'll have him under observation the whole time?"

"Just like today," Carter confirms. "The van will be swapped so that no one becomes suspicious, and it's parking spot changed. But we'll keep you informed," he assures Palmer.

"Just as long as you do," he frowns.

"Boss, I think you've got to let this thing happen," Craig tells Palmer in his deep laid back drawl. "This city has enough trouble without the likes of Jennings tryin' to rule the roost!"

"He's right...," Cartwright puts in, "...his kind are like a disease that takes hold and festers. It isn't just that he's breaking the law, he's corrupting the youth of this city. He's ruining their futures and hurting their families."

Everyone turns to look at Cartwright; it's the longest speech he's ever made and it sounded heartfelt.

"Sounds like you had some experience with this," Craig says quietly.

"My brother. It wasn't Jennings, but someone just like him," Cartwright admits. "I think that's why I joined the force – I want to get rid of his kind of scum!"

"We'll get him...," Carter assures the group, "...we just need to take our time and do it right. That way he won't squirm out of the charges, and he'll go down for a good length of time!"

By the time Craig gets home, Zoe has gone to bed. She's been turning in early more and more as her pregnancy progresses.

"Sorry, Carly," he smiles as he crosses the room to the woman who has stolen his huge heart. "The meeting was good but long."

"Come and sit down...," she encourages, patting the settee for him to sit next to her, "...was Sean ok? Did he get the information the police wanted?"

Nodding, Craig takes her tiny hand in his big one and raises it to his lips.

"He's got to continue with the pretence of working for Jennings for a while longer, but he seems happy to do it," Craig frowns. "He's a brave guy; he's doin' it all for his family. Apart from the fact that Jennings threatened them, Sean wants him off the streets to keep them safe for everyone!"

"You admire him," Carly states knowingly.

"Yep, I do," Craig smiles and nods his large head. "But right now I'm thinkin' more about you – I can't tell you how much I love you, Carly. You've given me more than I could have hoped for."

Twisting up on the settee, Carly reaches a hand to touch his cheek. "The feeling is mutual. I'm happier than I ever imagined I could be. And that's all down to you."

Outside the lounge door, Zoe smiles and creeps back up the stairs to bed.

Every day she looks out for Palmer coming into the office. One time she missed him when she nipped off to the loo, and she hasn't seen him since.

"Craig, how come Palmer isn't in the office more? I was hoping to get a moment with him," she tells him hopefully.

"He's still working out all Connor's business," Craig explains.

"Executor stuff?" she asks.

"Yep. His life was far from straight forward. It's down to Palmer to settle it all."

Watching Craig disappear into Palmer's office, Zoe wonders what there is to settle.

It's been 6 weeks since Connor died, but it feels like 6 days. The dreams are easier to cope with now, but I still miss him terribly.

Only 11 weeks to go before Brook is born, Connor. I'll be sure to share my photos and memories of you with her as she grows up.

I miss you, Connor.

Just then, Palmer strides into the room and Zoe starts guiltily.

"You ok?" he asks, watching Zoe's hand fly to her stomach.

"Yes, yes, I was just... I'm fine," she stutters, wishing she hadn't just been thinking about his brother.

"You sure? You don't look so good. Maybe this work idea wasn't a good one!"

"I'm fine!" Zoe asserts more forcefully. "And I enjoy being back at work. I just...I've been wanting to talk to you, but you haven't been around much lately."

"I suppose you want to know about the photos," Palmer guesses, unable to hide a look of disgust. "Well you can read the results for yourself, I'm busy," he tells her, taking a manila envelope out of his inside pocket and dropping it on to her desk before striding away into his office.

Staring at it, Zoe contemplates reading the contents then understands just what her mother had been telling her.

It is important for her to show Palmer that she trusts him, and not because of any lab report. *I have to convince him. But he doesn't look like he's in the mood to listen.*

Oh lordy, what have I done! He's the father of my unborn child and it looks like I've pushed him away once too often.

"Alright, Craig, I'll let you know how it goes," Palmer says as he steps out of his office and closes the door.

When he looks at Zoe she is still staring at the envelope having not touched it at all.

"It won't bite," he tells her stiffly. "I thought you'd be dying to read it. It's what you've wanted, isn't it?"

But Zoe sadly shakes her head as she looks up at him.

"I don't need it."

"You..." Palmer looks aghast, then closes his eyes in exasperation. "After everything, you don't even want to see the truth."

Snatching the envelope up, Palmer makes to leave, but Zoe calls him back.

"I don't need it because I believe you," she pleads quickly. "I think I always have, I just didn't trust myself to be right."

For a long moment he just stands and stares and Zoe is convinced she's too late.

"What are you saying, exactly?" he asks, moving back to her desk.

Rounding it to stand beside him, Zoe hopes he can see the truth in her eyes as they plead for forgiveness.

"I was so wrong. I have no excuses, and I know I don't deserve your forgiveness, but I'm asking for it anyway," Zoe tells him, then draws in her bottom lip to stop it from trembling.

The wait seems interminable, then his hand reaches up and he draws his thumb along her bottom lip, freeing it from her teeth.

His kiss is gentle yet possessive, flooding her with relief and love.

As it deepens their souls touch and entwine, eternal lovers back where they belong in each other's arms.

<u>CHAPTER THIRTEEN</u>

Lying in Palmer's arms, Zoe can't believe the happiness she has been given. After all the trauma and lies the world seems bright and new and full of hope again.

"Was that a good sigh or a bad sigh," Palmer asks while stroking her hair.

"Definitely a good sigh," Zoe chuckles. "I'm so happy – I can't remember ever feeling so happy," she grins up at him.

"Me either," he tells her, returning her grin with one of his own. "Your mum and Craig sounded pretty happy too, when you phoned them last night."

"Yes. My mum has always believed you," she tells him, and watches his eyebrow lift in surprise. "She told me. And when I realised how wrong I have been she helped me to see what I had to do. But I was terrified that I'd left it too late, that you didn't want me anymore."

"I was hurt and angry, but I never stopped loving you," he tells her softly. "That just isn't possible. Ask Tara," he smiles cryptically.

"Tara! What has she got to do with anything?"

"Quite a bit, actually," then he hauls them both into a sitting position and tucks her under the crook of his arm. "Tara sees things. And she told me that you are my 'eternal wife'. It's the only reason she agreed to help me to win you back."

"She...that is so weird! And you believed her?" Zoe asks, stunned to think that Palmer is actually being serious.

"I do believe her," he corrects. "I've always known that what we have is special. I knew you were mine from the moment we met, it just took me a while to understand what I was feeling."

"I must admit, I felt drawn to you right from the off, but I thought it was just the way you put me at my ease. I was so nervous that day I came for interview, but you were lovely."

"I liked the way you fell for me," he tells her, and chuckles at the memory of her falling out of the lift and into his arms.

Batting at him playfully, Zoe joins in the laughter. "It isn't very gentlemanly of you to remind me of that."

"It isn't very gentlemanly of me to say that you are getting really big either...," he smiles lovingly, stroking his hand over her belly, "...but you are. And I've never seen you looking more beautiful."

"You're just saying that," she reprimands with a playful frown.

"No, I'm really not," Palmer insists, not playful at all now. "Can you imagine how it feels for a man to look at the woman he loves and see her happy to carry his child in her womb. There is no greater beauty than that."

Tearing up, Zoe covers his hand on her belly with her own and moves it to where Brook is moving.

"I think she heard her daddy's voice," Zoe whispers, and looks at him with all her love in her eyes.

"We're going to be parents," Palmer speaks quietly, reverently. "That's amazing."

"I'll be 30 weeks at the end of this week," Zoe informs him proudly. "I have a hospital appointment tomorrow; you could come with me...if you want to," she offers falteringly.

"It would make me so proud," Palmer says, gently turning her face towards him. "I love you so much, and I can't wait to meet our daughter."

Then he sees a shadow pass over here face and wonders if she is thinking of Connor.

"Palmer, I know you went to a lot of expense for a wedding I didn't stick around for," she begins hesitantly. "But I wish I had. I'm sorry."

Glad that he hadn't voiced his suspicions, Palmer hugs her to him.

"I don't care about the money, only that we didn't get married," he tells her. "We'll put that right after the baby's born."

"Actually, that's kind of what I'm saying," and she draws herself up to a sitting position, watching him carefully for his reaction to the suggestion she's about to make. "I want to get married before Brook is born. I don't want her to be born out of wedlock," Zoe affirms, both hands cradling her swollen womb.

Heaving a large sigh, Palmer leans back into the pillows. "I know I'm good, but even I can't organise a wedding in less than 10 weeks."

Shaking her head, Zoe looks at him earnestly. "You and me, Palmer. Just you and me and a couple of witnesses, that's all I want. But more than anything, I want to be Mrs Zoe Johnson on the day we have our baby."

For a long moment he just looks at her, then breaks out in a loving smile.

"That would be precious," he tells her. "But I doubt your dad could get over here at a moment's notice. Would you mind?"

But she's already smiling and shaking her head. "He's already here. We haven't spoken properly in so long I haven't had a chance to tell you," she laughs happily. "My dad is renting a house and he's staying till after Christmas. It couldn't be more perfect!"

"Ok. That's great!" Palmer agrees. "So that will be Carly and Craig, my mum and dad, and your dad." Then he cringes a bit, "Might be a bit awkward."

"No. Not at all. My dad is happy for mum," she pronounces proudly. "He told me that he lost his chance but that mum deserved someone to love her and take care of her. He seemed to like Craig, the more I told him about them."

"Are you sure about this," Palmer frowns with concern. "We were going to have a beautiful wedding, now you're suggesting we get married in a register office with just our parents and Craig."

"That's all we need," Zoe smiles and touches his cheek. "And I only need you. I've been such an idiot."

"Ok. I'll get right on it," he chuckles happily. "Now I'm going to get us some drinks to celebrate with."

And with that, he leaps out of the bed and makes his

way, completely naked, over to the kitchen.

"You have one fine body," Zoe tells him lasciviously. Then she laughs when Palmer wiggles his firm backside.

Coming back to the bed he passes her one of the champagne glasses that he has filled with orange juice.

"To us. To our eternal marriage – may we forever find each other."

Then they chink glasses and take a sip of the juice.

"This is the best champagne I have ever tasted," Zoe tells him with a grin.

"Well, we'll have the real thing after Brook arrives. Then I'll take you on a long honeymoon somewhere romantic," Palmer tells her, and is surprised to see her look troubled by his suggestion.

"But...what about Brook..."

"What? She'll come with us, of course!" he tells her as if it was a foregone conclusion. "We'll wait until she's about six months old then we'll take off for a few weeks. Somewhere not too hot, and we can teach her to build sandcastles."

"That sounds wonderful," Zoe agrees, relieved that he wasn't suggesting they leave Brook behind.

"We're a family, Zoe, we don't go anywhere without each other. Right?"

"Right," she agrees happily, and they chink glasses

again and finish their orange juice.

The following day at the antenatal clinic, Zoe sits holding Palmer's hand while waiting her turn to be seen by the midwife.

"I think we're next," she smiles up at Palmer happily.

A couple of minutes later, a heavily pregnant woman vacates the midwife's office and Zoe hears her name called.

"We're up," Palmer smiles, standing and helping Zoe to her feet.

"Hi, how are we doing?" Jan, the midwife asks Zoe, and shares her welcoming smile with Palmer to include him in the conversation.

"I think we're doing fine," Zoe bubbles happily. Then, knowing the routine, she slips off her shoes and lays on the examination table, waiting for the midwife to proclaim her fit and healthy again.

Lifting her smock top to expose her abdomen, the midwife starts to feel her stomach this way and that.

Then she gets the Doppler, a small electronic device for listening to the baby's heartbeat.

"Ok, just a little gel and then we'll start," Jan tells her as she smears the gel on her belly.

The volume on the Doppler had obviously been left on high and a loud electronic squeal reverberated in the room when first the probe was put into the gel.

Quickly, Jan twiddled a knob and the squeal was silenced to a more manageable grumble.

"That's better. Now then, the baby's heartbeat should be somewhere around here," Jan muses as she moves the probe on Zoe's stomach. And then the miracle of their baby's heartbeat can be heard loud and strong.

Holding Palmer's hand, Zoe looks up at him with tears in her eyes and sees that Palmer too looks choked up.

"She sounds strong, like her daddy," Zoe tells him, and feels him give her hand a gentle squeeze.

But he doesn't speak, he can't, his throat is clogged with emotion.

"I'm not happy with these ankles," Jan proclaims, tearing them out of their wonderful moment. "Are you on your feet a lot?"

Zoe sees Palmer frown and turns her attention back to the midwife.

"No, not at all. I've just returned to work because I was getting bored stiff being at home all the time, but I'm sitting mostly," Zoe tells her hopefully, but doesn't dare look back at Palmer.

"That's just as bad," Jan frowns at her. "Sitting with your feet down still allows fluid to gravitate down to your ankles. And, indeed, I would recommend that you get up and walk at regular intervals to help your circulation."

"So, what do you advise to take care of this problem?" Palmer asks with concern.

"Well, if you must work you need to take regular breaks where you can sit with your feet raised up to allow the fluid to naturally drain back into your circulatory system," Jan informs them with a smile. "That should do it."

"Then I'll make sure that's what happens from now on," Palmer states decisively.

When they get out to the car, Zoe turns to Palmer with a plea in her eyes but he heads her off before she can utter a word.

"Zoe, I've allowed you to continue working at the office against my better judgement, but that won't continue if you don't do as the midwife tells you," he frowns as he backs the car out of the parking space and heads towards his office.

"Damn it! I'm going to look like a fool if I sit at my desk with my feet up all the time," she grimaces.

"You don't need to sit that way all the time," Palmer reasons. "Just ten minutes in the hour should do it if you do it every hour, I would think."

"Well hark at the expert!" Zoe snaps and folds her arms over her baby bump.

"Now you're acting like a child!"

Then suddenly and inexplicable, Zoe burst into tears.

"Zoe? What the hell?"

Pulling the car over to the side of the road, Palmer unsnaps their seatbelts and pulls Zoe into his arms.

"Don't cry, baby. I'm an idiot – I know nothing about these things, I'm just trying to look after you," he croons as he strokes her back. "And now I've made you cry, I'm sorry."

"I don't know what's wrong with me," she mumbles into the wall of his chest. "I'm not even that upset, I just can't stop crying."

Palmer frowns over the top of her head, wondering if this is normal.

"I'll take you home," he offers gently. "You can come back into the office tomorrow if you feel up to it."

With some relief he feels her nod against his chest and pulls back to survey her face.

"Are you ok?" he smiles hopefully.

With a shudder that goes right through her, Zoe nods and takes the tissue that Palmer is holding out to her.

"I think I just got all emotional when we heard Brook's heartbeat and this is me letting it out," she tells him after blowing her nose.

"That was a very special moment," he recalls with a

proud grin. "I've never heard anything so beautiful or so full of life."

"I know...," Zoe finally smiles, "...it's like she's saying 'hello, I'm really here just waiting to meet you'."

"Yes, well, let's not hurry the process," Palmer frowns again. "You need to rest up a bit and take care of those ankles. I don't want a secretary with fat feet," he jokes, and gets a slap on his arm for his trouble.

"And I'm not your secretary anymore, I'm Craig's," she huffs playfully. Then she frowns up at him, "When are you coming back, I miss seeing you in the office."

Feeling a guilty jolt in the pit of his stomach, Palmer tries to brush it off.

"I still have a lot to sort out for Connor," he tells her. "We can't even read his will until his estate has been settled, so I need to keep working on it."

With some relief he watches her nod and smile. "Sorry. I was just being my usual selfish self. But I miss you," and Zoe tilts her face up for a kiss.

"It won't be long, I'm almost done." Palmer kisses her then leans across to refasten her seatbelt. "Give me a couple of weeks and all this should be behind us."

<u>CHAPTER FOURTEEN</u>

The first accident on the Dersinger building site was staged to look like one of the undercover officers had been hit on the shoulder by falling debris.

It was so convincing that Sean pales when he sees the blood supposedly oozing from a shoulder wound.

"Jesus! Are you alright," he asks, panicked by how much blood he can see.

With a snigger, Cooper groans dramatically then winks at Sean. "I'm fine, the stuff you kicked off the scaffold missed me by a mile. But it looks good doesn't it," he smiles, then groans when one of the regular workers comes over to take a look.

Sean immediately sends him off to call an ambulance and the police are at the call centre waiting for the call to come in.

When the ambulance arrives ten minutes later, another officer is dressed as a paramedic and takes a look at the injured man.

"Can we clear some room please," he tells the men who have gathered around.

"He's right, get back to work and I'll deal with this," Sean tells them convincingly. "And be careful, we don't want any more accidents!"

Three days later another accident sees Rogers with his jeans ripped and his leg broken by a fall from the same scaffolding that the debris had fallen from injuring Cooper.

"What the hell happened?" Sean demands hotly as he stands over Rogers.

Laying on the ground writhing in pain, Rogers shields his broken leg from view.

"The scaffold felt like it was giving way," Rogers groans. "I lost my balance and fell. Sorry boss, I think my leg's busted!"

"For christ's sakes, someone call an ambulance," Sean shouts, then crouches down next to Rogers. "Are you ok, son? That was some fall."

"No worries, I used a parachute roll to save my legs," Rogers confides. "The cuts and bruises will just make it look more authentic."

When the ambulance has gone, Sean calls all his men together and gives them a health and safety lecture.

"Now make sure you follow the rules and stay safe," he finishes angrily. "I want two of you experienced men to dismantle that scaffolding and then make sure it's put back together again properly. I will not have any more accidents on this building site, do you hear me!"

A rumble of assent rolls through the men as they disperse to do his bidding. But Sean notices a suit near the fencing and knows that Jennings will be apprised of his progress.

Yes, you go back to Jennings and tell him that I've been a good boy. No doubt he'll be thrilled to hear that two of my men are in the hospital. Though, thank the Lord, it isn't true!

When Craig and Palmer both show up on site, none of the men are surprised.

They talk with the two men who are dismantling the scaffolding and get their opinion about what happened.

Then they go round the other men, asking what they saw and if there were any high jinks going on to cause the accident.

But everyone tells them that Rogers was just working one minute and on the ground the next. No one saw anything untoward or out of the ordinary.

"Ok, I appreciate that," Palmer tells the last of his men. "Just take care, alright."

Meeting up with Sean and Craig, Palmer closes the port-a-cabin door behind him as he steps inside the site office.

With a smile, he walks passed the other men and heads for the kettle.

"That seems to have gone over well," he smiles as he fills the kettle then plugs it in. "The men don't seem suspicious at all. Just worried about the accidents and how the men are doing."

"Yeah, Rogers and Cooper were popular," Sean tells them. "They had an easy way with jokes and were willing to help anyone out if they needed it. I think the men will actually miss them," Sean chuckles.

"So now it's up to Carter to get his men in here as Health and Safety Inspectors," Craig nods and takes the mug of coffee that Palmer is holding out to him.

"Here you go, Sean." And Palmer passes him a mug of coffee also. "When do you think that will happen?"

Sean frowns as he speculates. "Carter said they'd give it a few days so I'd say probably next week sometime."

"Hmm, they've carried it off so far, let's hope they're convincing when it comes to the inspection," Palmer muses cautiously.

"Yeah. And we need to visit our men in the hospital or Jennings will get suspicious," Craig's deep voice rumbles.

"Jesus! This is getting complicated," Palmer sighs, but nods in agreement. "I'll go now, supposedly to check on Rogers and then I'll visit Cooper."

"Visit him...?" Sean asks, his coffee almost to his mouth.

"Well I'll pretend to," Palmer clarifies.

"I'll be glad when this is all over. You should have seen the way Rogers fell off that scaffolding – believe me, no one would suspect he was faking it," Sean tells them. "He damn near gave me a heart-attack!"

"And Cooper told Carter you went white as a sheet when you saw all the pig's blood on his shoulder," Craig chuckles.

"Haha, have a good laugh," Sean smiles at Craig, taking it all in good humour. "But I can tell you, he looked like he was going to bleed to death it looked that real!"

"You're a good man, Sean," Palmer claps him on the back with a grin. "Maybe you should go into acting after this – I'll write you a good recommendation."

The three of them enjoy the light moment and finish their coffees.

"Ok, I'm off to the hospital to do my visiting duty," Palmer tells them. "Are you going back to the office?"

Craig nods and gets to his feet, seemingly taking up a great deal of room in the port-a-cabin. "We've had a couple more tenders accepted – I think we're finally back on our feet work wise."

"That's good to know. You ok here, Sean?" Palmer asks as they all step outside and walk through the building site.

"No problem, boss. I'll make sure everyone is extra careful from now on."

Zoe is so happy that she and Palmer are a couple again. When she'd told her mother what had happened in the office, Carly had been really pleased for them both.

Now she is sitting with her feet up on a chair with a cushion on it, feeling like an idiot.

Thank heavens no one is likely to walk in on me. This is ridiculous! But I have to admit, it is working.

The swelling around her ankles has greatly reduced and looks almost normal.

With a loving smile she thinks about Palmer and how caring he's always been.

I must have been crazy to believe he would ever cheat on me. Palmer just isn't that kind of man. He's so kind and so considerate, I really am lucky not to have lost him for good.

It still hurts to think of Laura being responsible for

delivering the hurtful notes that had started all the bad feeling between her and Palmer.

But she didn't fake those photos. So who did? I wonder if she knows?

The more she thinks about Laura and the notes, the more she begins to suspect Connor.

I really wish it wasn't true, but it's the only thing that seems to make sense.

Palmer said that Laura really believed that he was cheating on me, that she thought I had a right to know.

That means Connor must have convinced her by showing her the photos – but does that necessarily mean that he faked them?

What if someone gave them to him? Like, 'take a look at these – your brother's got a bit on the side'. That could happen.

But as much as she doesn't want to believe that Connor would have done such a thing, Zoe just can't quite convince herself.

Why, Connor? Why would you want to hurt me like that? You said you loved me, you said you'd take care of me and Brook.

And I believed you.

When the telephone rings it makes Zoe jump and put a hand to her racing heart.

"Johnson Construction, how may I help you," she recites politely.

"Zoe, I'll be there in half an hour to pick a few things up from the office. We can go out for lunch if you'd like," Palmer offers.

"I'd love that," she smiles into the phone.

"Ok, see you soon."

I wonder if Palmer has any ideas on the photos. They were very convincing. I have no idea how you would even begin to do such a thing. I imagine it would take special software and a lot of skill.

Hmm, I'll see how lunch goes then maybe I'll bring it up. I don't want to upset things with Palmer already.

When he arrives, Palmer is dressed in a business suit like he used to wear to the office.

"I haven't seen you in a suit for a while," Zoe smiles appreciatively when Palmer stops by her desk. "It reminds me how sexy my boss is."

"I hope you're not talkin' about me," Craig chuckles as he follows Palmer in.

"Oh! Craig!" Zoe gasps and blushes wildly.

Still chuckling, Craig continues into the inner office and leaves Palmer to talk with Zoe.

"You blush beautifully," he tells her, rounding the desk to plant a kiss on her lips.

"You could have warned me," she scolds him quietly.

"How did I know you were going to try to seduce your boss," he chuckles playfully.

"Go and get your things, I'm starving," she laughs when he tickles her ribs.

"You two sound real happy again," Craig smiles when Palmer enters the office.

"We are. No thanks to Connor," Palmer tells him without rancour.

"How's all that coming along," Craig asks as he leafs through a couple of files.

Making sure the door is still closed, Palmer looks worried.

"I don't think Zoe has put it all together yet. She knows about Laura and that it was Connor who convinced her to send the notes – but I don't think she realises that he had the photos made up."

"Hmm, I don't know," Craig muses, and leans back in his seat. "Zoe's no one's fool."

"But she hasn't said anything – at least, not to me," Palmer states with a raised brow. "Has she said something to you or her mother?"

"Nope. But Zoe is bright as a button and I don't think it will take her long to figure it out now that she's admitted to herself that you're innocent."

Heaving a sigh, Palmer says, "That was some uphill battle, I can tell you. Then, after all that, she doesn't even want to read the report. She's adamant that she doesn't need to know what it says."

"Well that's good, isn't it? At least you know she trusts you no matter what," Craig's deep voice rumbles quietly.

"I suppose. I just wish all this business with Connor was out in the open. I don't want to hurt Zoe, but I feel like I'm lying to her by not letting her in on what I'm doing."

"Hmm. Only you can know what the right thing to do is," Craig tells him wisely.

"But that's just it, I don't know," Palmer sighs, pushing his hands back through his hair. "I don't want to lose Zoe all over again just because she's got some idealistic view of Connor."

Their lunch goes really well, with Zoe and Palmer chatting happily and relaxing in each other's company.

"Have you picked out a dress for our wedding?" Palmer asks with a happy grin.

"Not yet, but mum suggested we go shopping together tomorrow. It won't be quite the same as the last time, but I'm still really excited," she tells him.

"Are you really sure about this," he asks again, still not convinced that a quickie wedding is what Zoe really wants.

"I've never been surer about anything." And reaching across the table she takes Palmer's hand. "I love you. All I want is to be your wife. I don't need all the trimmings."

"Well, if you're sure, I got a special licence for two weeks tomorrow..."

But he doesn't get to finish as Zoe lets out an excited scream. "Oh my gosh! That's amazing!"

But then she does something completely unexpected and bursts into tears.

"I thought you were happy," Palmer says as he rounds the table and takes a seat next to her. Putting an arm round her shoulders he holds her while she struggles with her tears.

"I am. I'm s.s.so happy," she tells him, and uses his handkerchief to wipe her eyes. "It's all I want – to be married before Brook is born."

"It really means that much to you?"

Nodding, Zoe tries to get herself under control and is grateful for Palmer screening her from the other guests.

"It means the world to me. I suppose it's old fashioned, but that's me," she smiles tremulously up at him.

"You're one on your own, alright. But that's what I love about you," he smiles as he touches her cheek gently. "That and the fact that you're all mine!"

Maybe now isn't the time to talk about Connor. Perhaps I can bring it up tonight when Palmer takes me home.

But when evening comes and Palmer picks her up from work, Zoe is hesitant to begin what could be a painful conversation for them both.

"Did you remember to put your feet up each hour?" Palmer asks as they pull out of the car park.

"Well...yes...and no," Zoe states with a side on glance at Palmer. "I sort of changed the rules a bit...to make it easier," she adds quickly.

"Zoe, you heard what the midwife said, you need to keep raising your feet up to let the fluid drain back into your circulatory system," he quotes, virtually word for word.

Zoe can't help a chuckle, then tries to straighten her face when Palmer glances a frown over at her.

"I'm sorry, and I am putting my feet up on the cushion you so thoughtfully provided," she tells him. "I'm just doing it every other hour to make it more practical for work. And it's working," she adds when he continues to frown. "I do 15 minutes with my feet up while I read the post or go through files and tenders," she explains matter of fact.

"And your ankles are ok?" Palmer queries sceptically.

"They are fine. You wouldn't know they'd ever been swollen," she tells him proudly.

"Then I suppose it's alright. But you need to keep it up or they'll get all swollen again," he warns, and Zoe loves that he's so concerned.

"I swear Brook is going to be a gymnast when she's born," Zoe laughs as her daughter kicks out and appears to turn over.

"Is she alright...nothing's happening is it?" Palmer asks anxiously.

"No...," Zoe chuckles, "...she's just trying to get comfortable. Either that or she's playing football with my intestines."

When they pull up at the traffic lights, Palmer reaches over to put a hand on Zoe's stomach.

"Jesus! Does that hurt?" he asks, wide eyed with wonder.

"No, but it can get a little uncomfortable sometimes. But nothing more than that," she explains. "I think the worst thing is the effect she seems to be having on my bladder lately. The midwife told me that it's a common problem as the baby gets larger and lays on the bladder. I swear I have to run to the loo at least once every hour. And I do mean run!"

Now it's Palmer's turn to chuckle.

"Sounds very problematic, but luckily you have a ladies room nearby."

"And a good job too," she tells him with a smile. Then the smile becomes hesitant as she deliberates whether or not to bring Connor up.

"Palmer, I've been thinking about Laura," she begins tentatively.

"Why! She wasn't a good friend to you, Zoe. You know that," he tells her quietly.

"I know she loved Connor and that she would have done anything he asked her to do," she states feeling a little braver.

"Yes, I think that's fair to say," he agrees.

"Then...Palmer, do you think it was Connor who made those photos? Or maybe someone gave them to him and said, 'hey, look at these'," she asks hopefully.

"What do you really believe, Zoe?"

For a moment she sits quietly, thinking about Connor and all he came to mean to her.

"I think the Connor I got to know in Cornwall would never have done such a thing," she tells him honestly, and hears him give a quiet sigh. "But the Connor who assaulted me in the car park would have." And folding her hands in her lap, Zoe falls silent and contemplative.

When they pull up at the front of her mother's house,

Zoe finally turns to Palmer.

"He changed, Palmer. I swear he couldn't have acted the way he did unless it was real."

Reaching over to cup her cheek, Palmer smiles tenderly. "I believe you. It sounds like Connor finally found himself in his relationship with you."

Covering his hand with her own, Zoe smiles hopefully.

"You don't sound too upset about that."

"Maybe if he were still alive and coming between us, I would be," Palmer admits. "But as things are, I can't begrudge him the happiness he found before his life was cut so brutally short."

With tears brimming in her eyes, Zoe says, "You are such a good man. I really don't deserve you."

"We deserve to be happy with each other," Palmer contradicts. "Neither of us did anything wrong. What happened, happened, now we have to look forward and enjoy what we've been given a second chance at."

CHAPTER FIFTEEN

When the Health and Safety Inspectors arrive on site, the men all become nervous.

"Hey, Sean, what's going on," one of the building crew asks to one side.

"They're just doing their job," Sean assures him. "You don't have anything to worry about if you're working safely."

But when he walks away, the young man doesn't look convinced.

Sean watches as he goes to another couple of builders and a discussion starts.

"Ok you lot, wait until you're on break to have your mother's meeting," he shouts over. "This job is far enough behind as it is!"

With a groan of acceptance, the men break apart and

get back to work. Then Sean watches the suits walk around his building site as if looking for evidence of bad practice.

If I didn't know better, I'd be worried. They're really convincing!

Watching them writing on a clip board, Sean wonders what they are finding to write about. After all, they are undercover policemen, not building inspectors.

A couple of hours later, Sean finds out.

"You got all this from being on that scaffold?" Sean asks in surprise.

"You'd be surprised what we can observe in a short space of time," Ben Webster tells him.

"Yeah, but they were really obvious," his colleague, Greg Blakesley shakes his head in disgust. "No wonder Jennings wants you on his crew, those two out there haven't got a brain cell between them."

Continuing to read their notes, Sean is shocked to see a mention of Jennings.

"You actually saw Jennings pull up and talk to them?" he asks in disbelief.

"He has a driver. He was in the back of his car, but when the window wound down and he spoke to his goons, he was clearly visible," Ben confirms.

"It's a pity you couldn't get that on camera," Sean sighs.

"We did," Greg chimes in as he puts the kettle on. "I got confirmation from our street guys a few minutes ago."

"So you're not the only police working this?" Sean asks, brows raised in surprise.

Ben chuckles softly. "Our Chief wants him real bad. We're watching him 24/7."

Impressed, Sean heaves a sigh of relief. "That sounds really positive. Hopefully it shouldn't be long before you take him in."

"That's the plan. We have a lot of tech guys listening in and recording conversations. The court order was difficult to get, but once it was explained who this creep is and what he's been up to, the judge signed off ok," Greg states as he brings three mugs of coffee over.

"So what happens now? Do you need to shut us down for a while, or what?" Sean asks.

"No," Ben answers promptly. "When we walk out of here we'll make a point of issuing you with an envelope that Jennings' men will assume is a legal document. Then we'll leave and see what transpires from Jennings' end."

"What are you expecting him to do?" Sean asks curiously.

"What we're hoping for is that he will ask his men to bring you to his office for further talks," Ben continues.

"Where we'll be listening in and backing you up all the time," Greg assures him.

"Ok, that sounds reasonable," Sean nods agreeably. "Are Palmer and Craig aware of the plan?"

"Yes. The only proviso they've asked for is to be informed prior to you going to meet Jennings," Greg explains. "They want to be on hand to give you their support."

"Yes, that would be typical of those two," Sean smiles. "They're hands on in anything they do, and they'll want to see to it that you're men are on the case."

Greg and Ben look at each other and smile. "Yes, Carter told us as much," Ben admits.

"Carter seems like a good man, I'm not worried that he won't have my best interests at the forefront of his mind," Sean attests easily. "But Palmer and Craig will be watching for anyone too intent on trapping Jennings."

"That's fair enough," Greg nods in agreement. "But I don't believe any of our men would put your safety in jeopardy to get to Jennings. That would make us as bad as him!"

A few minutes later they act out the handing over of the envelope that they had talked about.

"We will be back for a further inspection," Ben tells him officiously. "The measures stipulated in that document are not just recommendations, they are mandatory for this construction to continue. If we return to find that any of those measures have not been carried out, this site will be closed down. Is that clearly understood?"

Sean can feel the eyes of his men upon him as he walks with the two suited men to the edge of the building site.

Sure enough, just as Sean is locking up for the night, Jennings' goons walk up behind him.

"Mr Jennings wants to see you!"

No please or thank you, just an order issued and expected to be complied with.

"I have a family to get home to," Sean protests convincingly. "I don't want to be long or they'll start to worry."

But Sean goes with the men, knowing that Carter's men will have heard the conversation through his wire. He hasn't gone anywhere without it since his first meeting with Jennings.

What's a bit of embarrassment compared to losing my life. And they did promise not to record me at home unless there were suspicious circumstances.

When he walks into Jennings' backroom office, Sean plays up to his role.

"What's all this about?" Sean asks quietly, keeping a calm exterior but without grovelling.

"Take a seat," Jennings orders with a smile. "I just want a report on how things are going with the job I gave you."

"Ok," Sean settles himself into his seat. "The accidents got reported by an anonymous informant," he explains with a finger pointing into his own chest. "And today we got a visit from the Health and Safety Executive. Everything is going just as you wanted."

"Good. Good." Jennings nods happily. "Did they threaten to shut him down?"

Sean knows that his goons will already have told him as much, but he goes through the details of the visit just the same.

"They read me the riot act and said they'd be back," Sean smiles. "They gave me a list of changes that need to be made and told me that if they weren't carried out we could be shut down."

"That's good. That's very good," Jennings tells him as he leans back in his seat to regard his new employee.

"I've got plans for you, Sean. Big plans. Are you interested in becoming my second in command," Jennings asks, obviously feeling that he is bestowing some kind of honour on Sean.

"I told you already, I don't want to give up my job," Sean frowns. "But I don't mind doing work for you when you need something doing," he adds placatingly.

"And I told you that you could keep your damn job," Jennings sits forward in his seat again, obviously not pleased that Sean isn't overcome with gratitude at his offer of promotion.

"You don't work evenings or weekends do you! So you'll take charge when I need a job doing." He looks up at the two gorillas still standing behind Sean. "You've seen the calibre of my current staff, I need someone who can string more than one thought together at a time," he grimaces in despair.

"You must have better people in your organisations," Sean states matter of fact.

"Yes, and they're doing the jobs I pay them for. I can't pull them off at a moment's notice," he tells Sean, starting to get annoyed with the conversation.

"Do you want the job or not?!"

"You already know my daughter is in a wheelchair," Sean explains. "I can't be gone too much, my wife needs help. But if you just want a bit of help with jobs now and then, I don't see why not."

"You'll be taking charge of those jobs," Jennings emphasises, once again leaning back in his seat. "You have brains and brawn, I want to utilise them both!"

Nodding, Sean offers his hand across the desk to Jennings.

At first Jennings just looks at it, and then he smiles reaching out to shake it.

"Good man! I'll be relying on you!"

After being dropped off back at the building site, Sean pretends to be checking the site's security as he waits for Jennings' men to drive off.

Once they are out of sight another car pulls up and Carter gets out along with Cartwright, Palmer and Craig.

"Come on...," Sean tells them, undoing the chain on the gate and letting them onto the site, "...we'll go in the office out the way."

Following close behind, the men pile in behind him as Sean unlocks the port-a-cabin and steps inside.

Only then does he allow himself to heave a huge sigh of relief and sits down heavily in his usual seat.

"Very well done, Sean," Carter commends him with a hand on his shoulder. "You held up well and were very convincing."

But Palmer doesn't look very pleased by the turn of events.

"Yes, he did well, but this is getting out of hand. I don't want Sean getting in any deeper with the likes of Jennings," Palmer warns. "He's a bloody lunatic!"

"It's alright boss..." Sean begins, but Carter interrupts him.

"We have a chance to bring down a man who has single-handedly undermined this city for the last decade! He is suspected of ordering the deaths of at least 16 people that we know about – Christ knows how many there are that we don't," Carter scowls at Palmer. "If Sean can get on the inside we stand a chance of putting Jennings away for good!"

"I understand all of that...," Palmer nods, "...but I have to be concerned for my man. While I want Jennings taken down, I won't see Sean get hurt in the process!"

"We are backing him up all the way," Cartwright chimes in calmly. "Sean will never be on his own. That wire stays in place and gets checked regular until we have Jennings locked away." Then smiling over at Sean, Cartwright says, "Sean's our man too, now. He's one of the team that will bring Jennings down."

Watching Sean smile and nod, Palmer has to concede that it's his decision.

"I just want you to know that you don't have to do this," Palmer looks across at Sean with concern in his eyes. "You have nothing to prove to me or to the police. But it's your choice; I just want you to be clear on that before you make it."

"I won't deny it gets a little scary when I'm in his office," Sean admits. "But I can handle this, boss. I want to handle this. Ok?"

Closing his eyes on a sigh, Palmer nods his head in agreement.

"But I want you to know, Cassie will get her operation whether you do this or not," Palmer looks over at the best man on his books, next to Craig. "I'll make sure of that."

Sean looks gobsmacked.

"You'd do that for my girl, after what I did to you," he asks shame faced.

"I will do that, and it will be my pleasure."

Zoe is feeling particularly tired today and is taking a nap on her bed.

"She's feeling the strain," Carly tells Craig as they sit on the patio. "She'll never admit it, but work is wearing her out."

"Do you want me to cut her loose?" Craig asks with genuine concern.

"No. No, she'll be alright. But maybe you could suggest she reduce her hours," Carly suggests. "When I was pregnant with Zoe I worked right up to the end, but I had to and I was used to working all hours. Zoe hasn't had to do that and she's finding it tiring."

"Hmm," Craig frowns with a deep rumble in his throat. "I'll take care of it tomorrow, don't worry. I'll put it down to training someone else to take over for when Zoe goes on maternity leave," he smiles conspiratorially.

Reaching across, Carly puts a hand on his large arm. "You're so thoughtful. I thank God every day that you happened to be in Palmer's office that day. I never dreamed I could be this happy again. I love you, Craig. You're a seriously good man."

"You're my woman," Craig smiles and puts his large hand over Carly's, covering it completely. "There's nothin' I wouldn't do to see you and Zoe safe and happy."

A cough comes from the open patio doors, warning them that Zoe is up and about, then she steps out cautiously onto the patio.

"Are you two lovebirds fit for company," she asks playfully.

"Come on out here, Princess," Craig chuckles and pulls a chair out for her. "We're just sharin' the love," he grins, and watches Carly blush.

Zoe giggles happily, really pleased to see her mother and Craig getting on so well.

"I slept longer than I meant to," Zoe tells them. "Dad is sending a car for me in an hour and I need a shower before then," she yawns.

"Are you sure you're not doing too much," Carly asks, worried by her daughters growing fatigue.

"Well it's not like I'll be driving myself," Zoe reasons. "I haven't driven in ages; Palmer doesn't want me to because of the baby."

"And very sensible that is too," Craig nods and smiles. "But you should be fine to go see your dad. You need to make the most of him while he's able to be here."

"Exactly," Zoe grins appreciatively. "And we did spend the day together yesterday," she reminds her mother.

"Yes, we did...," Carly concedes, "...and it was lovely to have your help to pick out my wedding outfit."

"I got mine too, don't forget," Zoe reminds her, then watches a shadow pass over her mother's beautiful face. "Stop worrying. I'm really happy with the arrangements," she affirms. "Being married to Palmer is all that matters, I don't need all that fancy stuff to say 'I do'," she smiles happily.

"Dead right," Craig agrees quickly, cutting off any protests that Carly might make. "And we can make it special by celebrating as a family. There's nothing better than a good family do," he laughs jauntily.

"I suppose so," Carly agrees, then smiles when she sees that her daughter really does appear to be happy with the arrangements. "Now go and get ready, or the car will be here and you'll still be in the shower."

Getting up, Zoe stops beside her mother and bends to give her a kiss on the cheek.

"You're the best mum ever!" Then she goes inside to get ready and leaves her mum feeling proud and full up with grateful tears.

"Zoe's a great girl," Craig tells her, and reaches his hand over to take Carly's. "She takes after her mother."

"She's my heart," Carly murmurs softly.

By the time the black Mercedes pulls up outside, Zoe has finished blow-drying her hair and come down stairs.

Going out to the patio, she gives her mother a kiss goodbye and surprises Craig by kissing his cheek too.

"See you both later," she shouts, and heads out to the waiting car.

"Hi Lee," she grins as she gets in the front seat and sees him frown.

"Hello Miss Zoe," Lee nods formally. "Your father won't be happy with you sitting up front. He told me so the last time you did it."

"Oh Phooey," Zoe laughs happily. "I'm not royalty and don't want to be treated like them. I like sitting up front."

"Hmm," Lee replies non-committally.

"Stop worrying. I'll tell dad that I insisted. It's much nicer up here," she chuckles, and settles back to enjoy the ride.

CHAPTER SIXTEEN

"Hi dad," Zoe grins as she steps out of the car and waddles towards him.

Shaking his head at Lee, Douglas Benson smiles indulgently at his headstrong daughter.

"Don't blame Lee," she tells him as he bends to kiss her cheek. "I hate sitting in the back of that big car."

"I just want to keep you and my granddaughter safe," Douglas tells her, putting an arm around her shoulders to draw her inside the large house.

"You're just used to people doing as they're told," she chuckles and looks up to see him nod in agreement.

"You're right, though it looks like I'm going to have to get used to you doing exactly as you please!"

Once inside, Douglas rings for attention and asks for a pitcher of iced orange juice when a young lady appears at the sitting room door.

"What is with this weather...," Douglas sits and wipes his brow with his handkerchief, "...one minute it's a typical rainy day in England, then it's like being in the Bahamas!"

"Haven't you heard of Global Warming?" Zoe asks with a chuckle. "They say the weather is swinging between extremes because of it and we can only expect it to get worse."

"Cheery thought," Douglas frowns, putting his handkerchief back in his pocket.

"Now, how are you and Brook doing? You look healthy enough and you seem to have more of a spring in your step lately," he smiles.

"I'm so happy," she grins at him. "I can't tell you how happy I am, and it's all down to Palmer. Next week can't come soon enough!"

Trying not to frown, Douglas' expression ends up looking like a cross between a smile and a grimace.

"I know you said you're happy with the wedding arrangements, but it isn't too late to let me put on a spread in the dining hall then you can invite more friends," he offers again for the umpteenth time.

"Daaaad," Zoe drawls in exasperation. "Just let it be. Palmer and I just want to get married in an intimate ceremony with our family present. It's all we need. And it's all I want," she emphasises for his benefit.

"Ok. Ok. Did you at least get a special dress for the day?" he asks, accepting defeat.

"Mum and I went shopping last weekend; we both got special dresses," she grins happily.

When the young lady returns with the pitcher of iced orange juice and a couple of glasses on a tray, Douglas thanks her then pours some out for Zoe.

"Good lord, this is marvellous," she gasps as the freshly squeezed orange juice tingles on her tongue.

"I can't stand that packet stuff," Douglas smiles with satisfaction as he too takes a sip of the cold drink. "This is much more refreshing."

"I hope you at least have an electric juicer...," Zoe giggles, "...I have visions of that poor woman standing squeezing the oranges by hand."

"Aimee and her mother are terrific. They mostly manage to look after me and the house, though they get help once a week from an outside cleaning service," he clarifies. "This house is too big for anything less."

"What made you rent such a large place," Zoe asks, looking around at her grand surroundings.

"It's what I'm used to. And I especially liked that it has an indoor pool," he smiles.

"An...you didn't tell me that the last time I was here," she splutters in astonishment.

"You want to go for a dip...?"

"No, I don't have a bathing suit!"

"No problem, there's a stack of them in the changing room. They're all new, you can just pick one out," he offers.

"Tempting...," Zoe smiles, then grimaces as she rubs her stomach, "...but I'm not sure I'm up to it today. Brook seems to be laying funny. I think she must be on a nerve, I've been getting some weird niggles in my back."

Frowning with concern, Douglas takes another sip of his juice while he considers that piece of information.

I seem to remember Carly complaining of back problems when she was pregnant with Zoe. Can't remember if it was significant or not. Maybe I should ring her mother and ask the question - though Zoe looks healthy enough.

"Have you been to see the doctor?" he asks, sitting forward in his seat to look more closely at her. "This heat can't be too comfortable in your condition either."

"You can say that again," and she lets out a moan of enjoyment when she takes a long drink of her iced juice.

"There's more if you'd like it," Douglas offers, enjoying pampering his daughter. He'd offered to buy her a new car when he'd arrived back in England a couple of weeks ago. But, as Carly had rightly pointed out, she wasn't allowed to drive her old one so what would be the point.

"I'm ok, dad. It's just nice to be here with you, you don't need to fuss over me."

"I've missed out on doing that for quite long enough," Douglas tells his daughter firmly. "My own fault, I know, but I intend to put that right."

Seeing Zoe getting ready to have a daughter of her own, only brought the memories of him and Carly back all the sharper.

I was such a fool to let Carly go. And for what, a few weeks with a bimbo I'd been stupid enough to think I was in love with.

She was never a patch on Carly. None of them ever have been. But it's too late now. I've lost any chance to win her back. And Craig is a special fella. She seems really taken with him.

When he looks up he notices Zoe watching him and feels guilty for his thoughts.

"You didn't say if you've been to the doctor," he asks to distract her. "I think you should consider it if the niggles continue."

But Zoe just shakes her head. "I have an antenatal appointment on Thursday."

"But it's only Sunday; are you sure you should leave it that long?"

Before she can answer a knock at the sitting room

door precedes Aimee coming into the room. "Lunch is almost ready, Mr Benson. Would you like it serving in the dining room or on the back terrace?" she asks politely.

"What do you think, indoors or out?" he asks Zoe.

"Is the terrace shaded?" she asks cautiously, and when her father nods she smiles. "Then let's go alfresco. It's nice to take advantage of doing things outdoors while we can. You know what the weather's like over here – we can get all four seasons in one day!"

"That's the truth," Douglas laughs easily. "And I have to admit, I've missed that a little."

"You've missed the rain and snow?" Zoe asks in disbelief.

"Yes. Constant sunshine can get boring," he assures her.

"Hmm, this heat has been exhausting. I do really enjoy the breaks when we get them," Zoe concedes. "Though let's pray for sunshine next weekend. I'd like to have a few nice family photos of my wedding day," she chuckles.

When Aimee gives them the nod, the two of them walk out to the rear terrace and take a seat at the table.

"This looks lovely," Zoe smiles brightly at Aimee having surveyed her plate.

"Yes, very nice," Douglas comments as he takes his seat.

"Thank you," Aimee smiles, pleased that they are happy with their meals. Then she disappears back to the kitchen.

"So how come Palmer couldn't make it today?" Douglas asks his daughter with a frown.

"I told you dad, he's got a lot on at the moment. But he sends his apologies and said he'd try and make the next trip. He really wanted to be here," she assures him sincerely.

"Well, let's hope he can find time for his own wedding next week!"

Zoe giggles, loving the way her father just has to get another 'dig' in about the wedding.

"At least we agreed to have it here," she reminds him. "You can't say fairer than that."

Her father lets out a harrumph sound that makes her laugh.

"Come on, dad, it'll be a great day; unless you're determined not to enjoy it." She looks at him, one eyebrow raised and waits.

"Of course I'll enjoy it," he smiles testily. "I just think my daughter should have a memorable wedding day. Is that so wrong?"

Reaching across, Zoe puts a hand on his arm. "I love that you care, but my wedding day will be memorable for all the right reasons this time. I'm finally going to marry the man I love."

Covering her hand with his, Douglas looks into her soft brown eyes. "I know you're right. You two belong together, it's plain as day."

Palmer is having a rough day. He's been going through the file that he obtained from the offices of the PI Connor hired.

At least Grady kept his documentation in good order. It looks like he's a meticulous man when it comes to his work.

Reading through the many reports, Palmer finds it harrowing stuff. To think his brother had been involved with all this without him knowing is a bitter pill to swallow.

I should have seen some signs that he was going so far off the rails.

Closing his eyes after reading about the surveillance Connor had ordered on him, Palmer sighs deeply.

Looking back, I did see the signs, but I was too stupid to realise what they were telling me. Connor was getting more and more angry and stressed, and I just wrote it off as more of his jealousy of me.

What an idiot!

And what will Zoe make of all this? I've tried to spare

her feelings, but it's going to be impossible to hide all this when she moves in next week.

The whiteboard, with all its information intact, has been packed away and stowed under the bed. As far as Palmer can see, they've worked out all they can from it – but he's reluctant to wipe it clean just in case.

Padding over to the kitchen, Palmer puts the kettle on and makes himself a strong cup of black coffee. He's been reading and working through Connor's finances for hours now, and his brain is starting to fog.

I just hope Zoe's had a better day than me. It's amazing how close she's become with her dad – I'm not sure I could be so trusting.

With a frown, he goes back to the job of unravelling Connors life and finances.

At least he was thinking of Zoe at the end. He's made sure she's financially secure, anyway.

It feels somewhat ludicrous that his brother had stolen from him to give it all away.

You may not have picked my pockets directly, but you took the work I should have had to secure my own men's futures. Didn't you think of that when you copied those tenders? Or were you so wrapped up in what you wanted that you didn't care!

Damn it, Connor! We were brothers!

When Monday dawns bright and early, Zoe gets up and into the shower.

She'd had a really good night's sleep and felt refreshed.

The sun was shining and she was raring to go – feeling the best she had in a while.

"You look cheery," her mother smiles when she makes her way into the kitchen. "Take a seat and I'll get you some cereal – what do you fancy?"

"Thanks. I'll have cornflakes, my stomach is a bit wobbly for anything sweeter."

"Are you not feeling well?" Carly asks, and scrutinises her daughter with concerned eyes.

"I'm fine. Better than in a long time," Zoe smiles easily. "And I slept like the dead."

"Ok. Well, I remember that wobbly feeling in my stomach when I was pregnant with you," Carly tells her. "Staying away from anything too sweet is a good idea."

When Craig enters the kitchen and sits at the breakfast table with Zoe, she grins up at him.

"What?" Craig frowns uncertainly. "Have I got shaving cream on my face?" he asks, wiping at his chin with his large hands.

"No. I'm just happy to see you," she chuckles. "Aren't you used to females smiling at you?" she asks playfully.

"Hmm," he rumbles softly. "Carly, is there something on my face?" he asks, still not convinced.

With a laugh, Carly brings over the bowl of cornflakes for Zoe and takes a look at Craig.

Then she bends to kiss him and smiles. "There is now," she tells him, and both women start to laugh.

"You did not just put lipstick on me," he protests, then wipes the back of his hand over his mouth. "I can't go into the office lookin' like a girl!" Then he frowns from one woman to the other as they both burst out laughing.

"No one would ever mistake you for a girl," Carly smiles, tearing off a piece of kitchen roll and cleaning off the last of the lipstick. "There, you're all manly and prime again."

"See...," he smiles at Zoe, "...your mother thinks I'm prime!"

Zoe shakes her head though continues to smile. "I can't help it if she needs glasses."

Then she shifts sideways quickly as Craig begins tickling her side.

"If you want a lift into work you best apologise," Craig tells her as Zoe jumps to her feet and away from him.

"Ok. Ok. I surrender," she giggles and retakes her seat. "You are a prime male specimen and I apologise for saying otherwise. There, do I still get my lift?"

"I'll think about it while I eat this delicious breakfast," he tells her while smiling up at Carly and giving her a wink.

Carly watches them tuck into their breakfast and gives God thanks for her present happiness. *I couldn't wish for more.*

The week passes uneventfully. Zoe is given a clean bill of health at her antenatal check-up, and the building site doesn't appear to be having any further problems. But Palmer can't shake the feeling that something is about to go wrong.

Why do I feel so uneasy? It's like the calm before the storm. I know I'm nervous about the ceremony, but this feels different. I just hope everything goes as Zoe wants it; I love her so damn much.

Zoe, however, is not nervous or uneasy at all. Her stomach has a few butterflies flitting around in it, but she's more excited than nervous.

Her mother had stayed over with her at her dad's house and Craig had gone over to Palmer's first thing this morning.

"It looks a little dull," Carly frowns out of the dining room window.

"It'll be fine," Douglas assures her. "I looked at the weather report and it said clear skies with lots of sunshine."

Crossing to the hotplates, Carly helps herself to bacon, scrambled eggs and a few mushrooms.

"You've been really good about all this," Carly tells him. "Hosting a wedding at such short notice isn't easy. Thank you," she smiles sincerely.

"It's my pleasure. Zoe has been kind enough to forgive my mistakes and let me back into her life, it was the least I could do," Douglas nods and smiles at his former wife.

If I could go back and undo my foolishness, I would. The stupidity of youth is boundless. But I'd give up all of my success if I could go back to being married to you.

When Zoe enters the room she sees the look that passes between her parents and hesitates to break the spell.

Not that she thinks anything is going on between them. But they obviously still care.

"I'm hungry as a horse," she declares, going to the hotplates and helping herself to scrambled eggs and a couple of rounds of toast.

When she sits at the table her parents look at her and grin.

"What? I am!"

"We can see that, dear," her mother chuckles. "It's good to see your appetite returning."

"I thought you'd be more nervous," Douglas observes as Zoe tucks into her food.

"No, not really. I've been looking forward to today and just want to get it over with," Zoe tells them, looking from her father to her mother with round excited eyes.

"You...just want to get it over with? That isn't how I hoped you'd feel on your wedding day," Carly observes with a frown.

"I don't mean it like that. I just want to be Palmers wife so badly. We've had so many things come between us, I just want to get it done. Signed, sealed and official, so nothing else can go wrong!"

"That isn't likely to happen now," Douglas assures her. "The Registrar should be here around noon and the wedding is scheduled to start shortly after that."

Putting down her knife and fork, Zoe heaves a loud sigh.

"I'm so happy, and so glad that today has finally arrived. I've been on tenterhooks all week," she grins happily.

"It's going to be a beautiful day," Carly agrees. "And look, the sun is shining, so now it will be perfect."

Zoe sits back and smiles serenely. "It could rain buckets and it would still be perfect!"

Her mum and dad look at each other, and after a moment of stunned disbelief they both laugh.

"You really have got it bad," her dad tells her. "But

that's good to know. Yes...that's very good to know."

Getting into the shower, Zoe scrubs at her long auburn hair and tries to think what she's going to do with it for the wedding.

I suppose I should make an effort to put it up, but I know Palmer likes it loose.

As her arms are stretched up to rinse the suds from her hair, Zoe feels that uncomfortable niggle in her back give her a sharper jab.

Damn it, not today! I want to be able to enjoy myself, I will not rest up and put my feet on the settee – which is what my mother and Palmer will demand I do if they catch wind of my discomfort.

No, I'll just take my time and it'll go away. No one has to be any the wiser!

Towelling off, Zoe gives her lower back a bit of a massage then goes through to the bedroom.

This place is beautiful. It's not exactly a mansion but it's blooming big! And just look at the garden. Dad must have a gardener, I can't imagine him pruning the roses or mowing the lawn. My dad is a Hollywood movie star. Hah! That is so funny, he's just dad to me.

I'm so blessed to have him back in my life.

Pulling on her bathrobe, Zoe sits down at the dressing table to begin the task of blow-drying and straightening her hair.

A knock on the door precedes her mother coming into the room

"I'd like to do that for you, if you'll let me," Carly offers as she crosses the room.

"That would be lovely," Zoe smiles up at her mother. "I remember you doing it when I was a child. It doesn't seem that long ago."

"No, it doesn't." And Carly has to swallow a tear as her heart clenches painfully.

"Mum, this is a happy day, you can't go crying at my wedding," Zoe rebukes gently.

But Carly shrugs of the emotion that threatens to swamp her and forces a bright smile.

"Lots of mothers cry at their daughter's wedding," she states matter of fact. "I'm not ashamed to say that I want to hold on to my little girl a while longer. But I know that's selfish of me, and I wish you all the luck and love in the world. Not that you'll need it, you and Palmer are so good together."

"Thanks mum. And you are never selfish," Zoe insists with a smile.

For the next couple of hours they enjoy some mother and daughter time. Carly finishes Zoe's hair and then they discuss makeup and the finishing touches.

"You dad has some beautiful roses in the garden, I

could make you a little posy to hold for the ceremony and maybe pin one in your hair at the side," Carly offers.

"That's a great idea, mum," Zoe smiles gratefully. "I was sort of wondering what I'd do with my hands."

"I'll go and see to that while you put on your makeup, then I'll get myself ready and we'll be all set!"

"Thanks mum. And tell dad thanks too. I've tried to say it already, but he just brushes it off," she explains as she watches her mother move to the bedroom door.

"I will. Now get a move on, we have a wedding to get ready for!"

CHAPTER SEVENTEEN

While Zoe is upstairs getting ready, her mother and father are making sure that the stage is set for their daughter's big day.

No matter what Zoe has said, they are determined to make it beautiful and memorable.

To that end they have arranged for a florist to make up swags of flowers and an arbour for the happy couple to stand under while they take their vows. No effort has been spared and the effect is simple but stunning.

The florist and her helpers have set the stage, and even brought with them a table decoration for the wedding meal that will take place after the service.

Just the family; a small intimate service and meal shared with loved ones.

With a few surprises along the way.

When Palmer and Craig arrive Carly beams with pride. "Don't you two look handsome," she declares. "I'm so glad we booked a photographer, I shall enjoy looking back at this day with a lot of pride and joy."

Craig crosses to plant a kiss on her delicately painted lips.

"You look beautiful," he smiles, taking in her duck-egg blue summer dress and hat.

"Thank you, kind sir," and she dips into a playful curtsy. "But you two need a finishing touch. I have buttonholes for you over here."

Douglas has already been fitted with a yellow rose in the buttonhole of his suit jacket and now Craig and Palmer have matching ones.

"I have one for you too," Carly smiles at a young boy who is standing next to his older sister. "There now, you look just like the rest of the men. And these are for you," she tells the young girl, handing her a matching posy of yellow roses. "They look lovely with your dress, do you like it?"

The young girl nods shyly, then peers up at her mother. "When will we see Zoe?"

"It won't be long now, but remember to stay quiet, we don't want to give the surprise away," her mother tells her with a conspiratorial smile.

Douglas disappears inside and goes up to Zoe's bedroom.

"Are you ready, sweetheart? Palmer's waiting for you," he tells her, then stops to take in the picture of loveliness before him.

"You look beautiful. Simply beautiful," he tells her, swelling with pride and holding his arm out for her to take.

"Really dad, I'm 32 weeks pregnant on my wedding day, I don't think that term applies," she chuckles, more than happy with the situation.

"It most certainly does, and I won't hear anyone say otherwise," he warns her. "Not even you. I'm very proud and honoured to be your father on this very special day, and for every day that follows."

Standing at the top of the stairs, Zoe reaches up to place a kiss on his cheek.

"And I'm proud to be your daughter," she tells him sincerely. "Now let me hold on tight; those nerves you were talking about earlier appear to be kicking in."

With a hand to her stomach, Zoe makes her way down the stairs carefully. At the bottom, she picks up the posy that her mother has made for her and holds it in front of her.

"Now I feel like a bride," she giggles nervously, then

grimaces when the twinge in her back gives her a sharp jab.

"Are you still having problems with your back?" her father asks with concern.

"It's nothing, but it does give me a jolt now and then," she admits, taking the time to give it a rub.

Walking through the house, her father steers them outside to the waiting surprise.

"Tara!" Zoe screams with delight. "How did you get here; and Annaleigh and Jack too! Is Brian with you?" she asks, her eyes scanning around for Tara's husband.

"Sorry, no. He couldn't get time off work," Tara explains, then leans in for a hug. "You look great...," then Tara tips her head to one side, "...but there's something...are you ok?"

"I'm fine. Just a few annoying niggles."

With one brow raised, Tara regards her friend carefully. "And how long have you been having these niggles?" she asks quietly.

Douglas looks at his daughter with some concern and answers for her. "Zoe told me about them a week ago, and she'd been having them for a few days before that."

Frowning at her dad, Zoe turns to her friend and smiles reassuringly. "I'm only 32 weeks along, I have plenty of time before I need to worry about the baby coming."

But Tara won't be put off. "Zoe, baby's come when they're ready. Very few conform to a schedule that you and your midwife have worked out," she states firmly. "Now you tell me if those niggles get any worse or start moving round to the front. Ok!"

"Ok. Jees, can I please get married?" she grins happily.

With a heavy sigh, Tara nods. "But I'm watching you lady."

Before walking around the side of the house to the rest of the wedding party, Tara bends to her children and gives them a kiss.

"You two walk nicely in front of Zoe and her dad, ok?"

"Ok mum," they reply in tandem.

Standing with her father, Zoe hugs his arm and smiles at the children.

"I think we're all ready. Would you like to lead the way," she tells the children.

Annaleigh takes hold of her brother's hand and they walk slowly round the side of the house just as their mother had rehearsed with them earlier.

When Zoe turns the corner to the huge rear garden, her eyes shine bright at the sight that greets her.

There, under a perfect arbour decked in white flowers, stands Palmer and Craig with her mother and the Registrar. And fanning out from the arbour are swags of flowers held on delicate, white Y shaped posts.

"Oh dad, this is so perfect."

Patting the hand that is tucked through his arm, Douglas smiles proudly at his daughter.

"Even if it's just us, we wanted it to be as beautiful and as special as you are."

Holding her hand out to place it in Palmer's, Douglas moves to the opposite side of the arbour to Craig and her mother and stands beside Tara.

The tune of a lovely hymn is playing in the background and Zoe can hear birdsong nearby.

Standing next to Palmer, Zoe feels all the love they share wrap around them with ties that bind across the ages.

"Dearly beloved...," the Registrar speaks the opening line, and so the ceremony begins.

And just when he finishes, Zoe lets out a sudden gasp that has all eyes turned to her.

Tara takes a step forward, but hesitates when Zoe looks and shakes her head.

The Registrar looks from Zoe to Palmer and then continues the ceremony when no one says otherwise.

Palmer and Zoe have chosen a more informal version of the marriage vows and Palmer gets to start.

Placing her wedding ring halfway onto her finger he says, "I, Palmer Johnson, take you, Zoe Benson, to be my lawfully wedded wife, my constant friend, my faithful partner and my love from this day forward.

In the presence of God, our family and friends, I offer you my solemn vow to be your faithful partner in sickness and in health, in good times and bad, and in times of joy as well as in times of sorrow."

Palmer feels Zoe grip his hand and hears a quiet gasp as he takes a breath then continues.

"I promise to love you unconditionally, to support you in your goals, to honour and respect you, to laugh with you and to cry with you, and to cherish you for as long as we both shall live."

Palmer pushes the ring all the way on to Zoe's finger and smiles.

For a moment everyone just watches Zoe as she catches her breath from a particularly nasty pain in her lower stomach.

"Zoe, what's going on?" Palmer asks quietly.

"Nothing. We're getting married, that's what's going on," she tries to smile, but it comes off more like a grimace.

The Registrar looks nervously on then tells Zoe to repeat after him, and she holds Palmer's wedding ring halfway down his finger and begins to make her vows.

"I, Zoe Benson, take you, Palmer Johnson... Oooh!"

she groans suddenly, clasping a hand to her stomach.

Everyone stops pretending that nothing is wrong and gathers around her.

"Zoe please...," Tara begs, "...I think we should get you to the hospital."

"What!" Palmer stares at her with shocked rounded eyes. "What's going on?"

"I think Zoe has gone into early labour," Tara tells him, and Carly comes to her daughter's side.

"Have you, Zoe? Have you been getting contractions?"

"How do I know...I've never been in labour before," Zoe grimaces. "I thought it was just backache. I've had that a lot lately."

"But it's changed, hasn't it?" Tara asks.

"I am not going anywhere until we're married!" Carly suddenly straightens and stiffens her spine, looking resolutely at the Registrar and then Palmer.

For a second everyone just stares, then Tara says, "Then let's hurry it along."

Taking a breath, Zoe takes Palmer's hand and repositions the ring then begins again as the Registrar gives her the words.

"I, Zoe Benson, take you, Palmer Johnson, to be my lawfully wedded husband, my constant friend, my faithful partner and my love from this day forward.

In the presence of God, our family and friends, I offer you my oooh-" she gasps again, but holds up a staying hand when someone makes a move. "I offer you my solemn vow to be your faithful partner in sickness and in health, in good times and bad, and in joy as well as in sorrow," she repeats quickly, trying to hurry the Registrar along.

"I promise to love you unconditionally, to support you in your goals, to honour and respect you, to laugh with you and cry with you, and to cherish you for as long as we both shall live," Zoe gasps out, using her hand to motion the Registrar to wind things up then pushes Palmer's wedding ring home.

Instead of going into his usual speech, the pale looking Registrar instead says, "I now pronounce you man and wife."

"We're married?" Zoe asks, stunned and almost disbelieving.

The Registrar actually manages to chuckle, though he still looks extremely nervous. "You are indeed. All you need to do now is sign the register along with your witnesses and the wedding is official."

The photographer has been taking photos all the way through; from Zoe and her dad coming down the stairs, the moment she saw Tara and her children and periodically throughout the service.

As they move to a table set out at the side with the register open and decked with swags of flowers, he captures the vital moment they all sign the register. And just in time.

"Right, that's it," Tara takes charge. "Palmer, you get Zoe to the hospital and we'll all follow behind."

In moments, a convoy of cars exits the drive leaving a gaping Registrar to see himself out.

CHAPTER EIGHTEEN

The maternity ward's waiting room is full of nervous energy. Tara is trying to reassure Douglas that his granddaughter has a good chance of being born ok, whilst keeping an eye on her own two children.

Carly was allowed to go in with Palmer and Zoe when she wouldn't let go of her mother's hand.

A nurse opens the door and the room stills with every eye turning to her.

"I have a note for Tara," she explains.

"For me?" Tara looks perplexed but moves to take the note that the nurse is holding out to her.

"It's from Mr Johnson – he was hoping you would be able to call his parents to let them know the situation," the nurse smiles encouragingly.

For a moment, Tara just studies her face, trying to read any worry in it.

"How are things going? This is Zoe's dad," Tara explains, holding a hand out in Douglas' direction.

"Your daughter is doing fine," the nurse assures him. "It is early for the baby but we have many successful deliveries at this stage, so please try not to worry."

Then she's gone and they are left to hope and pray that Brook will be one of those successful deliveries.

"Douglas, will you be ok if I just step out to phone Palmer's parents?" Tara asks.

"No problem. You go, the kids will be fine with me — won't you," he smiles down at the bored duo just as Jack is about to kick Annaleigh's shin.

"Behave!" Tara warns, then leaves them with a frown that could freeze hell over.

Ten minutes later when she returns, Tara finds her children in rapt attention listening to Douglas tell them about the movie he's finished making.

He mimics the sound of an explosion and his arms and hands fly wide to illustrate the effect. When Douglas turns to wink at her, Tara smiles at him and mouths the words 'thank you'.

Craig is sat by the far window, frowning down at his mobile.

"Something wrong," Tara asks, taking a seat beside the big man.

"No. Well, maybe," Craig's deep brown voice rumbles quietly. Then he chuckles, "I'm not sure. One of our men is helping the police to catch a very bad man, a criminal of the worst kind. We always figured we'd be there in the surveillance van when he had to go to a meeting with him, just so that we are nearby to offer support and... Well, I'm here," he frowns, lifting his hands and letting them fall into his lap. "And Palmer is where he should be, with Zoe and her mother."

"Which leaves you worrying about your friend," Tara nods in understanding. "And someone has let you know that this friend of your has to go meet this bad guy?"

Nodding his large head, Craig heaves a heavy sigh.

"And you're torn between your loyalty to Palmer and this friend who might need your help," she sums up for him, and again watches the gentle giant nod his head.

Pursing his lips, Craig continues to study his phone, reading the text that Carter sent him.

"If you give me your number I can keep you up to date with what's going on here," she offers, putting a supporting hand on his arm.

For a moment he looks brighter, then he frowns in thought and contemplation.

"Would Palmer want you to stay here or go support your friend?" Tara asks finally.

A couple of seconds pass before he answers, then Tara witnesses the sun shine in his eyes as he smiles at her.

"I know what Palmer would want," Craig nods with acceptance. "He'd want me to back up our friend, a good man with a family who wants him home safe. And I intend to see that that happens," he grins more easily now. Then he reads out his mobile phone number and watches as she taps it into her own.

"There, now, that wasn't so hard," Tara grins and pats his arm. "You go and take care of your friend. If Palmer comes out I'll tell him where you've gone."

But Palmer doesn't come out, and three hours after their arrival Tara decides she needs to take the children for something to eat.

"Why don't you come with us, Douglas? I'll leave my number at the nurses' station and ask them to contact us if there's any news."

He isn't hungry, but Douglas can see that Tara is genuinely concerned for him.

"Let's get an update first...," he tells her as he gets to his feet "...then we can decide. If Zoe is doing ok, I'd be glad to escort you and the children to lunch."

"Right you are," she smiles, and puts her arm through his as they walk ahead of the children to the busy nurse's desk.

"Excuse me...," Douglas gives the nurse his most charming smile, "...could you tell me how my daughter is doing. Her name is Zoe Benson," he informs her pleasantly.

A look of confusion crosses the young woman's face as she searches the board.

"We don't have anyone of that name on this ward. Are you sure you're in the right place?" she asks, then her eyes go wide. "Are you Douglas Benson...the film star?" she asks with an almost disbelieving look on her face.

But Douglas is only concerned for his daughter. "She must be here," he demands with furrowed brows. "We came in with her about three hours ago-"

Then Tara takes a step forward and again puts a hand to his arm, "You might have her under Zoe Johnson," she smiles, and turns to grin at Douglas. "Your daughter got married this morning – remember."

"Of course! Of course! Yes, look for Zoe Johnson," he tells the young woman, who, having rolled her tongue back up into her mouth, jumps to do his bidding.

"Yes, here she is," she sighs with relief. "She's still in labour, according to this."

"So, she's alright?" he asks hesitantly.

"Babies often take their own sweet time," she assures him. "As far as I know, Zoe is doing just fine."

Heaving a relieved sigh, Douglas turns to Tara. "Then it looks like we have a lunch date," he smiles, and winks at the children.

"Could I leave my mobile number in case you need to contact us?" Tara asks. "Her father would like to be nearby when the baby arrives."

The nurse happily takes down the details and promises to call if Zoe looks like she's getting close to delivering.

Then Douglas leans over the desk and places a gentle kiss on her cheek.

"Thank you, my dear. I'm very pleased to have met you," he smiles, and the nurse's jaw drops open again as she watches them head for the lift.

Before they step into the lift, Douglas and Tara hear the nurse let out a squeal as she tells a colleague that she's just been kissed by a 'drop-dead-gorgeous film star'!

"That was kind of you," she smiles up at Douglas as the lift doors close.

Having helped the children to choose a light meal, Tara and Douglas carry a couple of trays to a table in a more secluded corner.

Douglas tries not to attract attention, but still a few female faces turn their eyes to watch his progress across the restaurant.

"You've been recognised," Tara grins.

"I don't mind as long as they just look and let us eat out lunch in peace," he nods as they take their seats and dish out the food and drinks.

"Are you famous?" Annaleigh asks, turning to look at the women staring openly at Douglas.

"I make films, that's all," he dismisses lightly. "Don't let them bother you."

"So, you're a film star," she persists, as only a child can.

Douglas laughs and nods. "That's what they say. But really, I'm just Zoe's dad."

"Oh," she frowns, then tucks into her sandwiches.

"I've never thought about the day to day, but it must get difficult sometimes," Tara sympathises as Douglas keeps his head down to eat his food.

"I don't have a right to complain," he smiles undaunted. "It was my career choice and if they didn't like my films I wouldn't enjoy the life I have. So, most of the time I'm grateful to them." Then his smile turns into a grin, "Most of the time!"

"I'll bet," Tara chuckles, then looks a bit abashed as she makes a confession. "Actually, I'm a huge fan too. When Zoe told me who her dad was I almost fainted clean away."

"I love your accent, my dear," Douglas tells her. "And I love your straight talking ways. It's always a pleasure to meet a fan, especially one so beautiful and with such lovely children."

Enjoying their meal together, Douglas is glad that no one has actually approached him for an autograph or to chat.

Then Tara's mobile rings and he looks at her with startled, worried eyes.

"Yes, ok, we'll come right up," she tells the caller, then ends the call and looks at Douglas with eyes that give nothing away. "Ok you two, lets clear the table and you can take your drinks with you," she tells them while getting on with clearing things away.

"Tara, is Zoe alright?" Douglas asks quietly as he catches her hand to still her.

"I'm sure she's fine. The nurse just asked that we go up and speak with one of the doctors who would explain everything," she assures him gently.

Nodding silently, Douglas helps the children to collect their things and walks with Tara back to the lifts.

When they arrive back on the labour ward, the same nurse who had been on the desk when they'd gone to lunch is there to greet them as they return.

"What news?" Douglas asks, clearly worried about his daughter.

"Come with me," the nurse tells him, and walks ahead to a small office where a doctor is waiting to speak to him. "This is Mr Benson, Zoe Benson's father," the nurse introduces, then leaves the room.

"We'll be in the waiting room," Tara tells Douglas, and watches him nod absently.

"What's happened – is Zoe and the baby alright?" he asks again.

"Both are fine, at this stage," the doctor adds ominously. "But we have had to take Zoe to theatre for a caesarean operation."

"What the hell for – everyone has been telling me that Zoe is doing fine. Now you tell me she needs an operation," he demands fiercely.

"The baby is lying in a breech position, which is not unusual in itself at this stage of the pregnancy," he assures Douglas. "We even deliver babies feet first if everything is going well. But in this case there were signs that the baby was struggling. Its heart-rate dropped markedly during Zoe's contractions, so it was decided to do a caesarean to remove the baby as quickly and safely as possible."

"How long has she been in theatre?" Douglas asks, having gone pale with worry.

"She was taken to theatre just before you arrived just

now," the doctor explained. "We did try to wait, but it wouldn't have been wise to delay any longer."

"No. No. I'm glad for that. You did what was best for Zoe and the baby...," Douglas nods, "...I'm not important. But I'll be able to see her the minute she gets back?" Douglas asks, his eyes pleading for the doctor's agreement.

Then he lets out a sigh of relief when the doctor nods and smiles.

"That's good. That's very, very good," Douglas tells him, and rubs trembling hands over his moist eyes.

"Are you alright, Mr Benson?" the young doctor asks with some concern.

"I'm fine. Just a little shaken up, but not to worry," Douglas stands and holds his hand out to shake the doctor's hand.

When he enters the visitor's waiting room, Douglas sees Palmer and Carly, as well as Tara and the children.

"You look white as a sheet," Carly states, crossing the room to take Douglas' elbow. "Whatever did they say to you?"

"Pretty much the same as you, I imagine," Douglas sits heavily on the chair that Carly guides him to. "I just wish I'd been here to see her before she went down. I didn't get to see her," he mumbles distractedly.

A mobile phone rings out into the quiet room and Palmer reaches into his pocket to answer it.

"Craig, where the hell are you?" Palmer asks when he hears the big man's voice. "You're what?!" Palmer frowns at the floor as he begins to pace the room and forgets that Carly is listening. "You stay in the van if they have to move in, do you hear me!"

Then Palmer looks up to the ceiling, his agitated hand pushing back through his hair. "You'll stay back and let the police handle it. Craig, I want your word on this!" Continuing to pace back and forth, Palmer looks like he's going to crush the mobile phone in his hand.

"Jesus! You're a pigheaded son-of-a-bitch. At least make sure the police go in ahead of you. They're trained, you're not!" Palmer states fiercely.

The conversation continues for a couple of minutes, with Palmer becoming more and more agitated.

"Why the fuck did it have to be today. I can't leave Zoe – they just took her to theatre for a caesarean," he tells Craig, then listens as his friend assures him that he's where he's meant to be and not to worry about him.

"Just remember, Jennings won't hesitate to have one of his men take care of you if you get in his way," Palmer spells out the danger that his friend could be in. "If Sean can handle it and talk his way out, all the better. Don't go rushing in unless the police see no other option!"

Then Palmer slumps down into a chair and sits staring at his phone.

"Will you tell me what's happened?" Carly asks quietly, taking a seat beside him.

"It's Sean. Craig's worried that things are not going well with Jennings," Palmer tells her, knowing that Craig has filled her in with what's been going on.

"Sean's in with Jennings now?" Carly asks, her brow creasing with worry.

"Yes, and someone else. We didn't think of that. We didn't even consider that Jennings might have a partner," Palmer shakes his head in disgust.

"You're not like Jennings, how can you expect to second guess a man like that," she tells him with a comforting hand on his arm. "And Craig is sensible enough; he won't go rushing in unless Sean is in real trouble."

Palmer can only hope that she's right. If anything happens to Sean or Craig while he isn't there...

"I'll crucify Carter if he puts my men in harm's way!"

Carly knows they are more than mere employees to Palmer. He takes a personal interest in all his men, but especially those he is close to...like Craig and Sean.

CHAPTER NINETEEN

Tension in the observation van is running high. Everyone is listening to a heated exchange between Jennings, Sean and another man that seems to be Jennings' partner in crime.

"I don't know him from Adam; why should I take your word he's not a nark! I do my own background checks and he's too clean, I tell ya!"

They hear Sean's chair scrape back as he jumps to his feet. "I hope you're not calling me a nark, 'cause I don't like being called names as I haven't earned," Sean tells the man bravely.

In the back of the van, Carter speaks to Sean, though he knows he can't hear him. "Cool it down, lad. Get the situation back under control."

"Baxter, you listen to me or get yourself out," Jennings

growls, his anger restrained, but on the edge.

"Don't you give me orders," Baxter snaps angrily, and Carter closes his eyes as the argument spirals out of control.

"I brought you in on my operation, and I decide when you're out," Jennings tells Baxter. "And I decide who works for me, and who doesn't," he growls more quietly, and Carter can imagine Jennings giving Baxter a stony-eyed glare.

Then they hear the office door open and a scuffle break out.

"I'll gut you like a fish for this, Jennings," they hear Baxter threaten loudly, and then an ominous click like that of a flick-knife opening fills the van and everyone holds their breath.

For a very long second time seems to stand still, then Carter opens the back of the van shouting..., "Go. Go. Go," ...and all hell breaks loose.

Craig's heart is in his mouth as he follows the armed officers out of the van and into the pub where Jennings has his office in a back room.

Some of the patrons in the bar try to block their way, but the police are having none of it. Craig bulldozes his way through, knocking men over like nine-pins.

His one aim is to reach Sean before Baxter can turn on

him after he's finished dealing with Jennings.

Like a large grizzly bear, Craig slams through the door and reaches to pull Sean out of harm's way.

A loud groan rips from Sean as Baxter swirls on him, his eyes enraged and full of evil.

With Craig holding his collar, Sean feels himself lifted off his feet and finds himself on the floor outside the office door.

The police follow after Craig just seconds later, having been held up by the patrons in the bar. But what they see when they enter the office brings them up short.

Baxter has Jennings pinned up against the back wall with a knife to his neck and Craig is on the floor bleeding like a stuck pig.

Officers pile on to Baxter, pulling him away from Jennings and handcuffing both men.

But Carter and Cartwright drop to the floor beside Craig to assess his injuries.

"Is Sean ok, is he alright?" Craig gasps desperately.

"An ambulance is on the way. You'll both be fine," Carter assures Craig while applying pressure to the stomach wound.

"Don't look so worried, I'm not goin' anywhere. I'm gettin' married," Craig smiles, then falls into unconsciousness.

Palmer is pacing the hospital waiting room; it seems like a very long time since they took Zoe to theatre and he's growing more and more anxious.

"Is this normal...," he suddenly asks anyone willing to answer, "...do these kinds of operations usually take this long?"

Carly walks to his side and rubs his arm in a motherly gesture of reassurance. "It has been a while, but take comfort from the fact that no one has come to tell us that there have been any complications. It could be that she is taking longer in recovery – Zoe may already be out of the operating room and just taking her own sweet time to come round."

"You think? You really think that's all it is?" Palmer grasps onto that thought like a drowning man would to a life raft.

"I do," Carly smiles, then they all turn as a nurse enters the room followed by a man dressed in theatre scrubs.

The atmosphere immediately freezes, the tension almost palpable as the surgeon moves further into the room.

"Mr Johnson?" the surgeon asks, his face poker straight and serious.

"That's me," Palmer replies, his knees almost giving out under him.

He wants to ask if Zoe's alright, if Brook survived the operation...but the words won't come out. Once the question has been asked the answer can't be taken back, and he isn't sure that he's ready to hear the bad news clearly visible in the surgeon's eyes.

"I gather you are all family?" the surgeon glances around at small group.

"They are," Palmer confirms. "Please, just tell us what's happened, this waiting is killing me," he states before dropping into a chair.

"I'll just take the children out," Tara interjects quietly, and swiftly removes herself and her children from the room.

Douglas and Carly move to sit next to Palmer, while the surgeon and the nurse sit together opposite them.

"Sometimes the strain of an operation can take a toll on the heart that can't be anticipated," the surgeon begins, and watches the small vestige of colour drain from Palmer's face. "Zoe arrested while on the operating table," he explains gently.

Carly reaches for Douglas' hand and feels her own held tightly. But Palmer has frozen, his blood turning to ice at the surgeon's words.

"The situation is critical and that is why Zoe has been admitted to the Intensive care unit where you can visit with her as soon as we've finished here," he informs them. "Your daughter...," he continues with a soft smile, "...is doing really well. She weighed in at 7lbs 3ozs; a respectable weight for one born so early. But we've taken her to the neonatal unit for close observation overnight."

Zoe arrested. She had a heart attack. She almost died! She almost died! Oh God, what have I done! If she hadn't been pregnant with my child... Brook. Brook's alive. She's doing well. But her mother...my wife... Oh God!

"Mr Johnson? Mr Johnson..." the surgeon repeats when Palmer doesn't respond, "...your wife appears to be responding as well as we would expect at this stage. If you would like to see either her or your baby, this nurse will facilitate both."

But it's Carly who eventually responds.

"I think my son-in-law is in shock. If you could give us a minute, we'll come out when we've had time to digest what you've told us."

With a nod of understanding, the surgeon gets to his feet and moves to the door, followed by the nurse.

"If you have any questions, just let one of the nurses know and I'll gladly make myself available to answer them," he assures them before leaving them to come to terms with the dreadful news he's just given them.

The two men appear still and stunned, so Carly takes

it upon herself to make the first move and stands in front of them.

"Zoe is alive," she states firmly. "We need to get ourselves together and start supporting her in her time of need!"

Douglas lifts his head to look at Carly as if she's speaking a foreign language.

"For heaven's sakes, snap out of it," she demands forcefully. "Palmer, Zoe needs you; you can't fall apart like this!"

Christ knows she wants to, but Carly has to stay strong for her daughter.

Douglas puts a hand on Palmer's back and gives it a gentle pat.

"Come on, son, we'll go and see Brook first then we can tell Zoe how she's doing. Ok?" he encourages, getting to his feet and standing by Palmer until he does the same.

He doesn't utter a word, but follows Douglas and Carly as they all make their way to the baby unit.

When they look through the window at a row of babies a young midwife points to Brook and smiles happily.

Palmer can't take his eyes off her. Her little legs are thrashing around and her arms flailing all over the place.

"She has a good set of lungs on her," the midwife

who'd showed them the way tells them. "We're just keeping her overnight to be certain that she's flourishing, then she'll be moved into the main unit."

"And you're happy with her so far?" Carly asks when Palmer doesn't.

"As far as we can tell, she just wanted out and is none the worse for her early arrival," the midwife grins as they hear Brook's loud cry for themselves.

"I see what you mean about her lungs," Carly chuckles. "Just like her mother when she was born. There was no ignoring Zoe when she wanted your attention."

Giving Tara the keys to his house and car, Douglas tells her to take the children there and make them comfortable.

"The sat-nav is pretty basic; my address is in the address book and all you do is touch the screen and press start — it will guide you right to my door," he smiles reassuringly. "We don't know how long we'll be...," he smiles at the well behaved children, "...and I have some pretty incredible ice-cream in the freezer."

Annaleigh and Jack both brighten at the suggestion and happily tug on their mothers hands to go.

But she shakes them off and puts a finger to her lips to quiet them.

"Just one minute," she tells them quietly, then moves

to Palmer's side. "I'm so sorry that what should have been a happy day has been filled with such worry. But Zoe is a fighter, that's something I've learned over the last months. And she loves you very much. Give her your strength and she'll come back to you, Palmer," Tara assures him.

On the adult Intensive Care Unit, they are greeted by a nurse who introduces herself as Kerry-Anne.

"Hello, I'm Kerry-Anne, if you'd like to take a seat in here I'll ask one of the Consultants to come and speak with you," the Deputy Sister tells them as she shows them into a small room set out with comfortable settees and chairs. "If you'd like some tea or coffee I'll make it and bring it back with me," she offers, but all three shake their heads.

Taking a seat in the very same room where he'd been told about Connor's injuries, Palmer waits, with Douglas and Carly, for news of Zoe with trepidation in his heart.

When the door opens and the Sister reappears, she is followed in by a tall man who smiles a greeting.

In turn he takes the time to shake each of their hands then takes a seat next to the nurse.

"I'm very sorry to be meeting you under these circumstances," Dr Fielding tells them sincerely. "But what I have to tell you is all good so far," he smiles encouragingly, noting Palmer's lowered head lift a little at his words.

"Are you Zoe's husband?" he asks softly, then continues when Palmer nods. "Good. Good. Well, I'm pleased to say that Zoe has stabilised and appears to be recovering well. Arresting while under a general anaesthetic isn't as rare as you might think, though neither is it a common occurrence," he assures them.

"So, you think Zoe will make a full recovery?" Carly asks eagerly.

"I have every confidence that, all things being equal, she will," Dr Fielding smiles and nods. "To help Zoe, we have sedated her, inserted a breathing tube into her mouth and put her on a ventilator," then he holds up a hand when Palmer's head snaps up. "That isn't as bad as it sounds," he assures them. "I envisage taking her off it sometime tomorrow – her progress has been that good," he tells them.

"Ok," Palmer finally speaks. "Ok."

"Having said that, I don't want to minimise what Zoe is going through," Dr Fielding looks from one to the other of his rapt audience in turn. "It is possible that she could deteriorate, though I don't expect that to happen. But I do need to make you aware that Zoe isn't out of the woods yet."

Kerry-Anne watches as Carly tears up and quickly moves to hand her a box of tissues.

"Thank you," Carly mumbles, trying hard not to give in to her tears.

"I understand that the baby is doing well," Dr Fielding smiles encouragingly. "We'll reunite mother and daughter as soon as possible, I assure you."

"Can we see her?" Palmer asks quietly.

"Absolutely," Dr Fielding nods. "Sister will make sure that Zoe is ready for visitors and then come back and get you, alright? Is there anything else that you want to ask or need me to go over again?"

But all three shake their heads.

"Ok, well if you do think of anything I'll be on the unit for a while longer. Just let Sister know and she'll arrange for us to have another chat," he tells them as he gets to his feet.

Once Dr Fielding has left the room, Kerry-Anne again offers them a hot drink, but again it is refused.

"I won't be long," she assures them as she leaves them to think about what they have been told and goes to prepare Zoe for her visitors.

"This feels like déjà vu," Palmer frowns, his eyes glued to a spot on the carpet.

"No! This is not like Connor," Douglas tells him. "The

doctors obviously think Zoe is strong enough to recover from this. This is a different situation entirely!"

But as he watches Palmer, he can see that his words are hollow comfort.

The boy looks like he's been punched in the gut. This is the worst thing that could have happened so soon after his brother's death!

When Kerry-Anne returns, she is smiling and asks them to follow her onto the unit.

Thankfully, Zoe is in a different room to the one Connor had occupied; for some reason that would have been more than Palmer could bear. But even so, it is hard for him to look at his wife without the fear of losing her knotting painfully in his stomach.

Standing back, he allows Douglas and Carly to move in on either side of the bed to be near to their daughter. Palmer just can't seem to believe what his eyes are seeing.

CHAPTER TWENTY

The Accident and Emergency is buzzing like a swatted beehive.

Cartwright stands back as the doctors and nurses move in an organised dance around Sean.

He's lost a lot of blood from the gash that Baxter managed to swipe across his stomach before the big man had yanked him out of the way of the deadly flick-knife.

But the damage had already been done.

The only good thing that can be said, is the wound would certainly have been deeper had Sean not been moving backwards at the time it was inflicted.

He probably owes his life to Craig, and he's struggling to hang on to his own as a consequence. Jesus, the whole thing went pear-shaped in a heartbeat!

I don't know who that Baxter guy is, but it's going to

be my mission to put him down for as long as the law allows!

Another bag of blood is hung and connected to Sean; it's his third and the doctors are struggling to stem the bleeding from his gut.

"Ok, theatres are ready for us – let's get him up there and on the table as quickly as possible," one of the doctor's orders. And another seemingly chaotic dance begins.

A portable defibrillator and an emergency bag of tricks that contains essential emergency drugs are taken, and a whole host of staff move alongside the bed as it is steered into a lift.

Cartwright can only wonder that everyone seems to know their role in the proceedings and speedily gets on with doing it.

I don't know how they do it! My brain would be fried trying to remember all that. And I'm sure I'd be the one having a heart attack due to all the stress! What a bloody job!

They're lunatics for even doing it, but fantastic people too!

As he watches the lift close, Cartwright feels the buzz of the Adrenaline still pumping around his system begin to subside.

Taking a minute to come down, he makes his way back to the front desk and asks where Craig Stanley has been taken.

He's informed that Mr Stanley is already in theatre and that his colleague is in a nearby office waiting to speak to him.

Carter's face is a mirror of Cartwright's. They've both been to hell and back, watching Sean and Craig receive medical care.

"How the hell do we explain this to Palmer Johnson?" Carter asks when he sees Cartwright enter the room.

"No one knew about Baxter. He was a wildcard thrown in at the last minute – Jennings was the only one aware of him," Cartwright frowns as he takes the only other seat.

"But how did we miss him? We've been watching Jennings 24/7 for the last couple of weeks – how did Baxter get past us?" Carter demands angrily.

"As far as we knew, when he went in the pub he was just another punter; he was never identified as a player," Cartwright tries to reason with his boss's conscience.

"And that's my damned point!" Carter jumps to his feet and begins to pace the small room, making it feel even smaller.

"We don't have squat on that guy; he's a complete

unknown and he managed to stick two civilians in the time it took us to get to them," his rant continues. "He's not some fresh-faced greenhorn who suddenly lost it — he's a hardened criminal that we should have known about, that we should have protected Sean and Craig from, damn it!"

"We'll find out what went wrong," Cartwright assures him. "And when we do I'll be the one to explain it all to Palmer Johnson."

Carter stops his pacing and looks Cartwright dead in the eyes.

"That's a job we'll do together. We both talked Sean into helping us and promised him our protection. Now we'll have to take the rap for letting him and Craig down."

Cartwright looks at the floor, his mind turning over the recent events.

"Baxter is a cold blooded killer; that much is obvious. I think he could have been a replacement for Hickey," he suggests quietly, trying to straighten out his thoughts. "Jennings was short one hit-man after he off'd Hickey — maybe Baxter was meant to fill his shoes?!"

Nodding, Carter retakes his seat and muses over that suggestion.

"And maybe he brought him in from out of town; could be even Jennings didn't know who he was getting involved with," Carter suggests, and looks up to find Cartwright nodding in agreement.

"Baxter is so quick to violence I'll bet he's done time. We'll soon find out who he is and put him back behind bars."

"You can put money on that! And we have enough to put Jennings away for a long stretch too," Carter states firmly. "I just wish it hadn't come at such a high price."

Over 5 hours later, the two detectives are about to exit the hospital when they hear someone calling their names.

When they turn their heads to see who it is, they are both shocked to see Palmer Johnson and Zoe's parents walking towards them.

"What are you doing here?" Carter asks.

"I was about to ask you the same thing," Palmer frowns quizzically.

"Maybe we should find somewhere quiet to talk," Carter begins, but as he makes to walk towards the main desk Palmer grabs his arm and stops him.

"You tell me what's wrong?" Palmer growls, all the stress he's got balled up inside of him building into a red rage.

When Cartwright moves to restrain him, Carter puts up his hand and says, "No. He needs to know, and he has a right to be angry."

At that, Palmer tightens his grip and pulls Carter even closer.

"What exactly do I have a right to know?"

Without any ado, Carter tells him the bad news. "Sean had to go to theatre to have his guts repaired after a maniac slashed him while he was in Jennings' office."

If it was possible, Palmer pulled the detective in even closer.

"You tell me he's still alive," Palmer demands, so quietly that anyone other than Carter wouldn't have heard him, or the threat that lined his words.

"He is. He made it through the op' and is expected to make a full recovery," Carter tells him, not looking away from the steel in Palmer's eyes. "But Craig didn't. I'm sorry."

For one crazy moment Palmer stares at the detective like he's gone insane.

"Do you want to run that by me again?" he asks, not sure he's really heard or understood what Carter told him.

"It was Craig who saved Sean. We were held up by Jennings' men in the bar; by the time we got through Sean was lying in the hallway and Craig was on the floor of Jennings' office," Carter relays in a dull voice.

"You let my men get injured doing your fucking job!" he growls angrily, his voice rising along with his temper.

Holding his gaze, knowing what his next words are going to do to this man, Carter tells it to Palmer straight.

"He's dead, Palmer. Craig didn't make it through surgery."

Time seems to stop, then flash forward at an immense speed.

Palmer's fist is in Carter's face before anyone sees him move. But when he dives on top of Carter to continue the beating, Cartwright shoots forward to drag him off.

But it takes him and two other officers to do the job.

"You bastard! You filthy lying bastard!" Palmer shouts, not even aware of his surroundings or the fact that Carly has fainted.

With his hands cuffed behind his back, Palmer continues to seethe as Carter is helped to his feet and given something to wipe the blood from his face.

When medical assistance is offered, Carter just brushes it aside and walks over to face a very angry Palmer.

"We got it badly wrong...and when you've calmed down enough to listen, I'll explain exactly what happened," Carter tells him, while trying to stem the flow of blood from his broken nose.

"Get those cuffs off him," Carter demands of one of the uniformed officers still holding onto Palmer.

They look very unsure, but move to do their boss' bidding.

Once freed, Palmer rubs his wrists as he pierces Carter with a glare that would have put the fear of God into a lesser man.

"Go to a church if you want absolution...you won't get it from me!" Then Palmer turns to see Carly seated on a nearby chair with a nurse and a doctor in attendance.

Epilogue

One year later...

The sun is shining and Zoe chats easily with her father on the patio of his house.

"I love that you bought this place. You really liked it when you were renting so it's nice that you managed to talk the owner into selling," she smiles over at Douglas.

"And your mum loves it too," he grins happily. "It's days like today that make me realise what a lucky man I am," Douglas tells her as he watches Carly play with Brook on the lawn.

"I don't deserve her after what I did, but I'll gladly spend the rest of my life making up for it," he tells Zoe sincerely.

"You know mum wouldn't want you to feel like that," she smiles, reaching across the table to cover his hand with hers. "And I love seeing you both so happy. Mum waited a long time for you, it was obviously meant to be."

"And you and Palmer, are you ok?" he asks, having noticed some tension in the air between them.

Watching Palmer with her mother and Brook, Zoe's heart contracts with happiness.

"We're fine. Or we will be," she amends, taking a sip from her lovely fresh squeezed orange juice.

"Can you tell me about it?" Douglas asks, his brow furrowed with concern. "I'm not asking just to be nosy, I care a lot about you two. If I can help in any way, I will."

But Zoe shakes her head. "There's nothing anyone can do. Palmer just has to come to terms with some news we found out yesterday," she tells him, continuing to watch her daughter lap up all the attention she's getting.

Then Zoe turns to her father and sighs. "I'm pregnant, dad, and Palmer isn't best pleased."

"Well, I imagine he just wants to get the move over with," Douglas reasons sagely. "He most likely doesn't want you lifting things. You have to admit, it would have been better if you were in your new house first."

But Zoe just shakes her head. "That's not it. He didn't want us to have any more children, ever," she states unhappily. "But I'm glad it's happened; I don't want Brook to grow up alone. I know how that feels."

"You've got me baffled," Douglas admits, watching Palmer laugh with Brook as he tickles her tum. "Palmer's a natural father; it's obvious that he dotes on Brook. Why on earth wouldn't he be happy about having a brother or sister for her?"

"Because he's frightened for me," Zoe explains, her eyes soft and full of love for her husband. "It isn't that he doesn't want more children; he'd have a dozen if it didn't mean me giving birth to them," she sighs again.

"He's worried that I won't survive the birth. Even though the doctors have told him that they will monitor me very closely and that what happened before is very unlikely to happen again."

"Can't blame the man for that," Douglas sides with Palmer. "You gave us all a fright, and that's a fact."

"But that could have happened to anyone. And I've given up work now," Zoe pleads her case. "I've told him that I'll rest up and even accept the help of a nanny, if that's what it takes to please him."

Douglas contemplates his hands, remembering the harrowing events of one year ago. "I don't think it's all down to you," he reasons thoughtfully. "I think Palmer is going through a rough time at the moment because it's the anniversary of so much misery."

"He lost his brother and his best friend within a few

weeks of each other, and then he very nearly lost you too," he tells her bluntly.

"I know," she agrees readily. "And I'm trying to give him some space to grieve, but at the same time we need to move on with our lives. And there is no way I could ever terminate my pregnancy, so he just has to come to terms with it one way or another!"

Douglas' head snaps back to look at his daughter in shock. "Has Palmer suggested such a thing?"

"No...," she tells him honestly, "...but neither will he talk about the pregnancy. He just clams up and walks away."

"Give him time, Zoe. Just give him a bit more time."

A week later, Zoe is supervising the move from Palmer's loft flat to the house they chose together.

"Come on, Brook, let's put your toys away or they'll get left behind," Zoe tells the happy toddler.

"Do you want me to take that," Sean asks as Zoe seals the box up.

"Thanks, Sean. If it were up to madam here, these toys would never have been packed," Zoe grins.

"Do you want me to take her for a bit," Cassie asks, delighted to be helping out.

"That would be great, if you really don't mind," Zoe smiles at Sean's daughter.

"Come on, Brook, let's go and play."

"She's doing so well," Zoe tells Sean when he comes back up for more boxes. "I can't believe how well the operation went."

Watching his daughter playing with Brook gladdens Sean's heart. "It was hard work for her, but Cassie did everything she was asked, and still does her physio exercises religiously."

"You must be so proud of her," Zoe smiles at the young girl who is keeping her daughter entertained.

"I am. And I'll never be able to thank you and Palmer enough for all you've done," Sean tells her seriously.

"I know Palmer was just glad to help," Zoe tells him. "After everything that happened, Cassie was the one good thing that he hung on to. It helped Palmer as much as Cassie," she tells him honestly.

"Yes, I know he suffered badly after Craig died. It was so soon after Connor," Sean acknowledges with a nod.

"Has he told you that I'm pregnant?" Zoe asks, keeping her voice down so that Cassie doesn't overhear.

"He hasn't mentioned it," Sean says, surprised that Palmer hadn't shared his good news.

"He isn't pleased," Zoe confides. "He's worried that I won't survive the birth. He thinks I'm tempting fate too far."

"She thinks I'm worrying for nothing," Palmer tells him, making Zoe jump.

Sean nods, looking from one to the other and feeling in the way. Picking up one of the heavy boxes, Sean moves towards the open front door.

"I might be speaking out of turn but, it seems to me you two were given a second chance together. Things could have gone very differently, but they didn't," Sean tells them simply. "Haven't you suffered enough tragedy without going looking for it?"

Palmer watches Sean leave and has to admit that his friend is right.

"I'm sorry...," he says, turning to look at his precious wife, "...I know I'm acting like an idiot, but I couldn't bear it if anything happened to you. You're my life, Zoe. You're the reason for everything I do."

Standing, she moves into his arms and winds hers about his neck.

"According to Tara I'm your eternal wife," Zoe reminds him. "I'll never leave you, Palmer. Not ever. I love you too damn much."

Their eyes close and their lips meet in a kiss that says 'I'm sorry, and I love you too'.

Then they hear a giggle and realise that they have an audience.

Grinning, they pull apart and Zoe feels her heart lift as Palmer's smile stays in place.

Forever and always, our hearts will beat as one. Eternally wed, and always loved.

*****

If you have enjoyed reading this book, please leave a review at the place of purchase. Thank you.

www.susan-elle.com